Miss Callaghan Comes to Grief

Black Curtain Press
PO Box 632
Floyd VA 24091

ISBN 13: 978-1627551113

First Edition
10 9 8 7 6 5 4 3 2 1

Miss Callaghan Comes to Grief

James Hadley Chase

PROLOGUE

It was a hot night. Oven-heat that baked the sweat out of the body and played hell with the dogs. It had been hot all day, and now the sun had gone down the streets still held the stifling heat.

Phillips of the *St. Louis Banner* sat in a remote corner of the Press Club getting good and drunk. He was a long, thin bird, with melancholy eyes and lank, unruly hair. Franklin, a visiting reporter, thought he looked like a bum poet.

Phillips dragged down his tie and undid his collar. The long highball slopped a little as he groped to put it on the table. He said, "What a night! What's the time, Franky?"

Franklin, his face white with exhaustion and his eyes heavy and red-lidded, peered at the face of his watch. "Just after twelve," he said, letting his head fall back with a thud on the leather padding of his chair.

"After twelve, huh?" Phillips shifted uneasily. "That's bad. That's dug my grave good and deep. Know what I should be doin' right now?"

Franklin had to make an effort to shake his head.

"I gotta date to meet a dame tonight," Phillips told him, blotting his face and neck with his handkerchief. "Right now that babe is waiting for me. Is she goin' to be mad?"

Franklin groaned.

"Franky, pal, I couldn't do it. It's a low trick, but not on a night like this. No, sir, I couldn't do it."

"Break it up," Franklin pleaded, scooping sweat out of his neckband. "I want to freeze myself to death in a big refrigerator."

Phillips raised himself slowly. A look of faint animation came over his thin face. Drunkenly, he patted Franklin on his back. "You've got somethin' there," he said. "Gee! The guy's got brains. I've been doin' you dirt. Boy, you've certainly got somethin' there!"

Franklin pushed him away. "Sit down," he said crossly;

"you're tight."

Phillips shook his head solemnly. "Come on, bud, you've given me an idea."

"I ain't moving. I'm staying right here."

Phillips grabbed his arm and hauled him out of the chair. "I'm goin' to save your life," he said. "We'll take a cab an' spend the night in the morgue."

Franklin gaped at him. "Wait a minute," he said. "I ain't goin' to sleep with a lotta stiffs. You're crazy."

"Aw, come on. What the hell? Stiffs ain't goin' to worry you. Think how cold it'll be."

Franklin wavered. "Yeah," he said, clinging to the table, "but I don't like it. Think you can get in?"

Phillips leered. "Sure I can get in. Know the guy there. He's a good guy. He won't mind. Now come on, let's get goin'."

Franklin's face suddenly brightened. "Sure," he said; "it ain't such a bad idea. Let's go."

Out in the street they flagged a taxi. The driver looked at them suspiciously. "Where?" he demanded, not believing his ears.

Phillips shoved Franklin into the cab. "The County Morgue," he repeated patiently. "We're passin' in our pails. This is just a matter of convenience, see, buddy?"

The driver climbed off his box. "Now listen, pal," he said, "you guys don't want the morgue. You wantta go home. Just you take it easy. I'm useta handlin' drunks. You leave it to me. Where do you live? Now, come on. I'll have you in bed before you know it."

Phillips peered at him, then put his head inside the cab. "Hi, Franky, this guy wants to go to bed with me."

"Do you like him?" Franky asked.

Phillips turned his head and looked at the driver. "I don't know. He seems all right."

The driver wiped his face with his sleeve. "Now listen, you guys," he said pleadingly, "I ain't said nuttin' about gettin' into bed wid youse."

Phillips climbed into the cab. "He's changed his mind," he said mournfully. "I've got a mind to slosh him in the puss."

"Well, maybe you're lucky. I thought he'd got a foxy smell about him. I don't think you'd've liked that."

The driver came close to the window. "Where to, boss?" he asked, in what he thought was a soothing voice. "This ain't the time to fool around. It's too goddam hot."

"The County Morgue," Phillips said, leaning out of the window. "Don't you understand? That's the one cold spot in this burg, an' we're headin' for it."

The driver shook his head. "You'd never make it," he said; "they wouldn't let you in."

"Who said? They'll let me in all right. I know the guy there."

"That on the level? Could you get me in too, boss?"

"Sure. I could get anyone in there. Don't stand around usin' up air. Get to it."

Franklin was asleep when they got to the morgue. Phillips hauled him into the hot street and stood supporting him. He said to the driver, "What are you goin' to do with the heap?"

"I guess I'll leave it here. It'll be all right."

They stumbled into the morgue, making a considerable row. The attendant was reading a newspaper behind a counter that divided the room from the vaults. He looked up, startled.

Phillips said, "Hyah, Joe, meet a couple of buddies."

Joe laid down his newspaper. "What the hell's this?"

"We're spendin' the night here," Phillips said. "Just look on us as three stiffs."

Joe climbed to his feet. His big fleshy face showed just how mad he was. "You're all drunk," he said. "You better scram outta here. I ain't got time to horse around with you boys now."

The driver began to edge towards the door, but Phillips stopped him. "Listen, Joe," he said; "who was the swell dame I saw you with last night?"

Joe's eyes popped. "You didn't see me with no dame last night," he said uneasily.

Phillips smiled. "Don't talk bull. She was a dame with a chest that oughta have a muzzle on it, an' a pair of stems that cause street accidents. Gee! What a jane!" He turned to the other two. "You ain't seen nothin' like it. When I thought of that guy's poor wife, sittin' around at home doin' nothin', while this runt goes places with a hot number like that, I tell you, it got me."

Joe undid the counter-bolt and pulled back the little door. "Okay," he said wearily, "go on down. It's a goddam lie, an' you know it, but I ain't takin' chances. The old woman would just like to believe that yarn."

Phillips grinned. "Down we go, boys," he said.

They followed him down a long flight of marble steps. At the bottom there came to them a faint musty odour of decomposition. As Phillips pushed open a heavy steel door the pungent smell of formaldehyde was very strong. They all entered a large room.

The sudden icy atmosphere was almost too violent after the outside heat.

Franklin said, "Jeeze! There's hoar frost formin' on my chest hairs."

On one side of the room were four long wooden benches. Round the other three walls were rows of black metal cabinets.

Phillips said, "If you don't think about it you'd never know there were a lotta stiffs in those cabinets. I like comin' here. I jest sit around an' cool off, an' it don't worry me at all."

The driver took off his greasy cap and began twisting it in his hands. "That where they keep the corpses?" he said, his voice sinking to a whisper.

Phillips nodded. He went over to one of the benches and laid down. "That's right," he said. "You don't have to think about that. Just settle down an' go to sleep."

With his eyes on the cabinets the driver sat down gingerly. Franklin stood hesitating.

"I wonder if Joe would stand for me phonin' my girl friend to come on down," Phillips said sleepily. He shook his head. "No, I guess he wouldn't stand for it." He sighed a little and settled himself more comfortably. "Franky, put that light out, will you? It's tryin' my eyes."

Franklin said, "If you think I'm goin' to stay here in the dark, you're crazy. This place gives me the heebies. I don't mind stayin' here so long as I can see those cabinets, but in the dark—why, hell, I'd be thinkin' they might be gettin' out an' lookin' me over."

Phillips sat up. "What you mean, gettin' out? How the hell can a stiff do a thing like that?"

"I'm not sayin' that they'd do it. I'm sayin' what I think they might be doin'."

"Don't be a nut." Phillips swung his feet off the bench and got up. "Now I'll show you somethin'. Let's have a look at some of these guys."

Franklin backed away. "I don't want to see them," he said hurriedly. "This burg's spooky enough without lookin' at corpses."

Phillips went over to the cabinet and pulled out a drawer. It slid out silently on the roller-bearings. In the drawer was a big negro; his pale pink tongue lolled out of his mouth and his eyes seemed to be bursting out of his head. Phillips hastily slammed the drawer shut. "That guy was strangled," he said shakily. "Let's try another or I'll dream about him."

The driver edged close, but Franklin went over and sat on the bench. Phillips pulled another drawer open. An elderly man, his face covered with a good half-inch stubble of beard, came into view.

"You wouldn't think he was dead, would you, boss?" the driver said.

Phillips shoved the drawer to. "Naw," he said, "he looks like he was stuffed." He walked over to the other side of the room. "Let's have a look at some of the dames."

The driver's face brightened. "That's an idea, boss," he said. "Can you unwrap 'em?"

Phillips looked over at Franklin. "For Gawd's sake, did you hear that?" he said. "This gaul wants to see some Paris pictures."

The driver looked abashed. "Don't get me wrong, boss," he pleaded. "If you don't think I oughtta look, I won't."

Phillips was pulling open drawers quickly, peering inside and hastily shutting them. "Real hot numbers don't seem to die these days," he said regretfully. "All old dames here." He paused and pulled a drawer open further. "Say, this looks better. Hi, Franky, come an' look at this."

Franky got up slowly and came over, impelled by irresistible curiosity. They all stood looking down at the girl lying in the drawer. She had flame-coloured hair, that showed a darker brown at the roots. Her thin pinched face wore a tragic look of one who has missed the good things in life. Her lips were gentle in death, in spite of the almost pathetic smudge of the lipstick that smeared her chin.

Phillips pulled off the sheet that covered her.

The driver said, "Oh, boy!" and trod on Franklin's toes to get nearer.

She was slender, but firmly rounded. Her body was as perfect as the three men had ever seen.

Franklin took the sheet from Phillips and made to cover her again, but Phillips stopped him. "Let her lie," he said, "she does somethin' to me. By God! She's nice, ain't she?"

The driver said wistfully, "It'd take a heapa jack to play around a dame like that."

Phillips continued to stare at the girl. He pulled the tag of identification from its slot in the drawer and studied it. "Julie Callaghan," he read. "Age 23. Height 5 ft. 4 inches. Weight 112 lbs. Address not known. No relations." He pulled the tag out further. "Cause of death: Murder by stabbing. Profession: Prostitute."

He released the tag, which snapped back into its socket. "Well, well," he said.

The three men stood silently looking down at the figure in the drawer, then Franklin said, "You never can tell, can you? Here I was workin' up some sympathy for her, and she turns out to be a whore."

Phillips glanced at him. "What's the matter with that?" he said. "Can't you give her any sympathy?"

Franklin threw the sheet over her and closed the drawer. "You ain't one of those guys who tries to put glamour in that type, are you?"

"You've got the angle wrong. That dame's doing a job of work. Maybe it ain't a good job of work, but all the same, she's human, ain't she?"

Franklin wandered to the bench and sat down. "Come off it," he said, "that don't hold water. I'll tell you something. I hate these broads. I despise them. To me, that dame is just one more of 'em out of the way. She got what was comin' to her. She was too damn lazy and too damn brainless to do anythin' else."

Furtively the driver had opened the drawer again and was looking with fascinated eyes.

Both Phillips and Franklin took no notice of him.

Phillips said, "Some of these girls are forced into the trade, Franky. You ought to know that. Gee! You ought to be sorry for them."

"Don't talk a lotta bull. Sorry? That's a laugh. Listen, there's too much crap going around about forcin' janes into prostitution. If a woman don't want to do it, you just can't make her. They do it because they want the things in life the easy way. They've got what you want, and they make you pay for it. They give you nothing. They'll cheat you, rob you, lie to you, and they certainly hate you. They're a breed on their own. To hell with them!"

The driver said, "Maybe this was one of Raven's girls."

The two looked at him. "Why do you say that?" Phillips asked. "Are you sure?"

The driver closed the drawer regretfully. "No, I ain't sure, but he always had the best girls; and she's a honey, ain't she?"

Phillips looked at Franklin. "You're wrong, Franky. Some of these girls had a bad time. Raven's girls had a terrible time. It's hick-minded to group them all together."

"Who's this Raven you're talkin' about?" Franklin wanted to know.

Phillips exchanged glances with the driver. "So you don't know Raven?" he said. "Well, well! Where've you been all this time?"

Franklin sat down. "Okay, okay, I'll buy it, just so long as you'll stop this sissy talk about whores. Tell me."

Phillips reached for a cigarette. "Raven was quite a boy," he said, setting himself comfortably. "He came to this town about a year ago. As a matter of fact, one of our crowd, working on the old rag, first got on to him. It was odd how it started. Damned odd. If old Poison's wife hadn't gone off the rails, maybe Raven would still be operating right now. It happened this way...."

PART ONE

1

June 3rd, 11.45 p.m.

"Take me out for a little drive, Gerry darling," Mrs. Poison said as the music stopped.

Hamsley looked at the big bulk of wrinkled flesh and was appalled.

"It's such a very, very hot night, isn't it?" she went on, walking across the ballroom floor. "It'll be nice out in the car"—she gave his arm a little pat—"with you."

Hamsley wiped his face with his handkerchief. "Yes, Mrs. Poison," he said.

He knew what was coming. He'd seen it coming for the last week. He had a sick feeling inside him as he followed her steady march across the floor. He could see people looking at him and smiling to each other.

As he went past the band the conductor said something he didn't hear. He knew what it was, and it made him sicker than ever. At the door he tried to persuade her to stay. It was like pushing the sea back with his hands.

It was dark outside, cool after the heat of the ballroom. They stood on the top step, trying to pierce the darkness.

Mrs. Poison put her hand on his arm. He could feel her trembling. "Isn't it wonderful?" she said. "My, my, it makes me feel young again."

Automatically he said, "Don't talk such nonsense. You're a young woman." She and the other old women paid him to say things like that.

"You mustn't tell untruths. I'm not young, Gerry, but I'm not old. I'm in the best years of my life."

Hamsley shuddered.

Out of the darkness a two-seater slid up to them. The young mechanic got out quickly and stood holding open the door.

Hamsley felt completely trapped. She'd arranged everything.

The mechanic winked at him and made a sign with his hand. Hamsley climbed in beside Mrs. Poison, ignoring him. He could have wept with shame.

He said desperately, "It's cold out here. You sure you won't catch cold? Maybe we ought to get back."

"Oh no!" She gave a giggling little laugh. "It's cold now. But we'll be warm soon."

There, she had said it. He knew beyond any doubt now. His hand shook as he engaged the gears and let the clutch in with a jerk. "Where shall we go?" he said, driving the car slowly into the road.

"Go straight. I'll tell you." She leant against him. He could feel her soft hot body pressing into his shoulder. He drove down the road for a couple of miles, then she told him to turn off to the left. He could hear the tyres bite into the dirt road, and the trees overhead blotted out the sky.

She said suddenly in a hoarse voice, "Stop."

He pretended not to hear. His foot pressed down on the accelerator.

She said in his ear, "Gerry darling, I said stop. I want to talk to you." At the same time she reached forward and turned the ignition key. The car slid to a standstill.

Hamsley stared into the night, holding the wheel tightly in his hands.

Neither of them said anything for a moment.

"Gerry darling, you're a lovely looking boy," Mrs. Poison said. Her hand touched his.

Hamsley moved away from her. "I'm glad you think so, Mrs. Poison," he said. "I guess it's pretty kind of you to think that."

He could feel her quick breath on his face. "Yes, Gerry, you're the handsomest boy I've ever seen. I don't know what Mr. Poison would say, but I could be very kind to you."

Hamsley shuddered again. "Why, Mrs. Poison, I guess you're always giving me things. I guess you couldn't do any more."

"There's one thing I haven't given you, Gerry." Out of the darkness her voice sounded horribly harsh. "Gerry, I'm crazy about you. I'm mad about you."

She put out her hands and caught his head, pulling him

towards her. She began to kiss him furiously. Her wet mouth made him want to retch. He suddenly pushed her away, his hands loathing the feel of her breasts.

He said, "No. I'm taking you back. I'm—I'm not going to break up your home."

She came at him again. "Don't be a fool!" she said harshly. "Come here—don't talk!"

He pushed her back more violently so that she thudded against the side of the car. He could see her staring eyes in the dashlight. She sat there heaving and panting, looking as if she could kill him. Then her mouth opened and a thin, reedy scream came out of the slack cavity that went through his head like red-hot wires.

He fumbled with the door-handle, pushed the door open, and got out of the car. He didn't say anything. He just wanted to get away from her. So he ran into the darkness, leaving her still screaming.

2

June 4th, 5.10 p.m.

Jay Ellinger sat behind his battered desk and scribbled on his blotter. His hat rested on the back of his head and a cigarette dangled from his lips. His completed copy lay in a wire basket by his hand, and he was through for the day. He had nothing further to do, but he made no effort to leave the office. He just sat there scribbling and smoking.

The house phone buzzed and he looked at it without interest. "You're lucky, laddybuck," he said, reaching out. "Two minutes, and you'd've missed me." He scooped the receiver to his ear. A girl said, "Mr. Henry wants to see you." Jay made a face. "Tell him I've gone home," he said hastily.

"Mr. Henry said if you'd gone home I was to ring you.

"What's the trouble? Is there a big fire or somethin'?"

"You'd better come. Mr. Henry sounds awful mad." She hung up.

Jay pushed his chair back and got up. Henry was the editor of the *St. Louis Banner.* He was a good guy to work for and he didn't often get mad.

As he walked upstairs to Henry's office Jay searched his mind to find any reason why he might be called on the mat, but he couldn't think of a thing. There was that little business about the extra expenses last week, but surely Henry wasn't going to crib about that. Maybe he was getting sore about the way Jay belted Mendetta in the Rayson trial, but then he'd passed the copy himself.

He shook his head. "Well, well, let's see what's bitin' the old guy."

He pushed open the frosted-panel door and walked in. Henry, a big fat man in his shirt-sleeves, was pacing up and down his small office. His cigar hung in tatters from his teeth. He looked up and glared at Jay.

"Shut the door!" he barked. "You've been a long time coming."

Jay lounged over to an arm-chair and sat down. He hung his legs over one of the arms and shut his eyes. "I'm sorry, Chief," he said; "I came as fast as I could."

Henry continued to pace up and down, ferociously chewing his tattered cigar. "What do you know about Gerry Hamsley?" he barked suddenly.

Jay shrugged. "Oh, he's a nice kid. He dances at Grantham's joint. Gigolo—but a better type of the usual breed."

"Yeah?" Henry planted himself in front of Jay. "A better type, hey? Well, let me tell you that guy has started somethin' that will mean my job and yours as well."

Jay opened his eyes. "You don't say," he said. "What's it all about?"

"The little swine tried to rape Poison's wife last night."

"What?" Jay sat up, his face startled, then he remembered Mrs. Poison and suddenly began to laugh. He lay limply in his chair and howled with laughter. Henry stood over him, his face black with fury.

"Shut up, you coarse-minded Mick!" he yelled. "There's nothing to laugh about. Do you hear me? Shut up!"

Jay mopped his eyes. "I'm sorry, Chief, but damn it, you ain't swallowin' a yam like that? Gee! Is it likely? She's old enough to be his mother, an' she's as fat an' as ugly as an elephant."

Henry snarled, "Want me to phone Poison and tell him that? He's been on to me. My God! You ought to have heard him. He's in a terrible way."

"Well, what's behind it? You know as well as I, all that's bull. What's he want you to do?"

Henry struck the air with his clenched fists. "He wants Hamsley on a plate. He wants Grantham's joint closed down. He's yelling murder, an' he's got blood in his eye."

Just then the phone rang. Henry looked at it doubtfully. "That's him again, I bet," he said, lifting the receiver off gingerly.

From where Jay sat he could hear a sudden bellow come over the line. Henry winced and nodded to Jay. "Yes, Mr. Poison. Sure, Mr. Poison. I quite understand, Mr. Poison."

Jay grinned. It did him good to see his chief sweat. "Why, yes, Mr. Poison. He's here now. I'll tell him to come to the phone." Henry looked at Jay with a grim little smile.

Jay waved his hands frantically, but Henry handed him the phone. "Mr. Poison wants you," he said, and stood, mopping his face.

This was the first time that Jay had ever spoken to the proprietor of the *St. Louis Banner*. "Ellinger here," he said.

Something exploded in his ear and he hurriedly removed the receiver. Holding it almost at arm's length, he could plainly hear Poison's roar. "Ellinger? You the guy I pay each week to be my crime reporter?"

"Yes, that's right."

"Say sir when you speak to me, you young cub!" Poison bawled.

Jay grinned at Henry. He pursed his mouth and made silent rude signs. "Yes, Mr. Poison," he said.

"Get after Grantham, do you hear? I want everything you can find about him. Get after that swine Hamsley. I'm going to close down the 22nd Club and I'm going to break Hamsley. I want action. Get out now and do something. Now give me Henry."

Jay handed the phone back to Henry and sat back fanning himself with his hat.

Henry listened for a few moments with an agonized look on his face, and then the line went dead. He hung up gently. "The guy's crazy," he said miserably. "He's been on to the D.A.'s office. He's been on to the police. They can't do anything. Grantham's in the clear. His joint's respectable."

Jay scratched his head. "Why doesn't he give Hamsley in charge?"

Henry came round the desk and pounded the top of Jay's chair. "For the love of God, don't say a word about Mrs. Poison. No one's to know about that. Poison only told me because I flatly refused to touch Hamsley. I'm not supposed to have told you."

Jay grinned uneasily. "Sure, if that yarn got around, Poison would be laughed out of town. Surely, he doesn't believe it?"

Henry shrugged. "Of course he doesn't. It's the old cow that's causin' the trouble. Poison's scared to death of her. She's after Hamsley's blood—and you'd better find out why."

"Listen," Jay pleaded. "I'm a crime reporter. What you want is a nice private dick, not me. Let's get Pinkerton on the job. He'll turn up the dirt quick, an' we'll all be happy."

Henry scowled at him. "You heard Poison. Go out an' get busy. Don't come back until you've got something."

Jay got to his feet. "For cryin' out loud," he said. "If this doesn't beat anything that's ever come my way. What chance have I got to hang anythin' on Hamsley? Besides, he ain't such a bad guy."

Henry sat down behind his desk. "I'm warning you," he said seriously, "you've got to find something. If we don't give the old man what he wants, we'll be out. I know him when he gets like that."

Jay stood by the door. "But what?" he said. "What am I likely to find? Grantham's all right, ain't he?"

"As far as I know. I hate to say it, Jay, but if you don't find something, we'll have to frame those two guys. I'm getting too old to look for anything else."

Jay shook his head. "Not on your life," he said. "I ain't framing anyone because Poison's wife thinks she's young again. I'll sniff around. If nothin' shows up I'm resigning. But I ain't framin' anyone."

Henry sighed. "Perhaps you're right," he said. "Anyway, for God's sake dig hard."

"I'll dig all right," Jay returned, and went out, shutting the door behind him.

3

June 4th, midnight.

There was a cop at the street corner, standing watching the traffic, swinging his night-stick aimlessly.

Raven saw him as he came out of the alley, and he stepped back hurriedly into the shadows. Obscenities crowded through his brain, and his thin wolfish face twisted with frustrated rage.

The cop wandered to the edge of the kerb, hesitated, then began to pace down the street.

Raven edged further down the alley, further into the sheltering darkness. He'd let the cop go past. Across the road he could see the large block of apartments with their hundreds of brightly lit windows. On the sixth floor, Tootsie Mendetta had a six-room suite. From where he stood Raven could see Mendetta's windows.

He stood against the wall, his head thrust forward and his square shoulders hunched. He looked what he was, a bitter, screwed-up thing of destruction.

The cop wandered to the mouth of the alley. Raven could see him looking carelessly into the darkness. The cop took off his cap and blotted his face with a large white handkerchief. It was a hot night. Standing there, his mind dwelling on a long, cold drink, he was completely unaware that Raven waited so patiently for him to go away. He put his cap on again and moved on past the alley, on towards the bright lights, towards the cafe where he could bum a drink on the quiet.

Raven gave him a few seconds, and then he walked to the mouth of the alley and glanced up and down the street. He saw nothing there to alarm him, and squaring his shoulders he stepped into the light of the street lamps.

In his apartment Mendetta amused himself with a pack of cards. He held a cigar between his thick lips and a glass of whisky-and-soda stood at his elbow. He played patience.

The apartment was silent except for the faint shuffling of cards as Mendetta altered their position. He liked patience, and he played with tense concentration. He heard Jean, in the bathroom, drawing off water, and he glanced over at the clock on the mantelpiece. It was just after twelve.

The phone suddenly jangled. He half shifted his bulk, his brows coming to a heavy frown, and stared at the phone.

Jean called from the bathroom, "Shall I answer it?"

He got up and walked with heavy steps across the room. "No, no. It'll be for me," he said, raising his voice so that she could hear. He picked up the receiver. "Who is it?"

"That you, Tootsie? This is Grantham."

Mendetta frowned. "What's the trouble?" he said sharply. "This is a hell of a time to ring me."

"Yeah, but this is a hell of a spot we're in." Grantham had a cold, clipped voice. "Listen, Tootsie, that little punk Hamsley's dropped us right in it."

"What are you talkin' about?" Mendetta sat on the edge of the small table, which rocked under his weight. "Dropped us where?"

"Hamsley's been digging Poison's wife. He's been playin' her for a sucker for weeks. She's spent a heap of jack on him."

"That's what he's at the Club for, ain't it?" Mendetta demanded impatiently. "Ain't he givin' you a cut?"

Grantham laughed bitterly. "It's not that. The old siren fell for him, and he couldn't take it. She took him out last night and tried to rape him. He ran away, the yellow punk."

Mendetta's fat face relaxed a little. "Well, what of it? You can't hold the boy up for that. Hell! I've seen that dame. She'd turn anyone's stomach."

"That so? Well, know what she's done? She's squawked to Poison. Said Hamsley's tried to rape her. How do you like that?"

"She's crazy. Poison ain't goin' to believe a yarn like that."

"No? Well, let me tell you he's hoppin' mad right at this moment. Maybe he doesn't believe it, but she's got herself in such a state, she does. That's enough for Poison. She's makin' him get mad. Listen, Tootsie, this is serious. Poison's goin' to try an' close us up."

Mendetta sneered. "Let him," he said. "What the hell do we care? They've got nothin' on us. He can't close us up."

Grantham cleared his throat. "You don't know Poison as well as I do. He'll attack us in that rag of his. He might turn somethin' up."

Mendetta considered this. "Not as long as I'm alive," he said at last. "I'll go round an' see that guy. We'll give him Hamsley, but he's got to lay off us."

"Will you do that?" Grantham sounded relieved. "Get round tomorrow early, Tootsie. This ain't the time to he down on it."

Mendetta stood up. "Leave it to me," he said. "I'll fix him," and he hung up.

Jean came out of the bathroom. She looked strikingly beautiful in her silk wrap. Perhaps her mouth was too large, but it gave her a generous look that was not in her nature. She was tall, with square shoulders, a narrow waist and thick hips.

"Who was it?" she said.

Mendetta went over to the table and gathered up the cards. He didn't feel like patience any more. "Grantham," he returned, putting the cards carefully in their container. He was a very tidy man. He took two little sips from the whisky.

She looked over at the clock. "What did he want? It's late."

Mendetta nodded his big head. "I know," he said. "Go to bed. I'll come in a little while."

She turned her head so that he couldn't see the sudden vicious look that came into her eyes. "Don't be so secretive," she said lightly. "Is he in trouble?"

He stubbed out his cigar. "He's always in trouble. That's why I'm here—to pull him out." He plodded over to her. His big heavy hand rested on her hip. "Go to bed. I shan't be long."

"Tootsie, I must know," she said. "Has something happened at the Club?"

He looked at her with a curious expression, half angry, half amused. He turned her towards the bedroom door. "It's nothing," he said. "Go to bed," and he smacked her across her buttocks very hard.

She went away from him, her knees weak and her inside coiled into a hard ball of hatred. She went across the bedroom to the window and pulled back the curtains. Leaning against the window-frame, she looked down into the street below. She remained like that for several minutes before she regained control of herself. If Mendetta had seen her expression as she stood by the window he would have been uneasy. As it was, his indifference to her feelings prepared the way for what eventually happened.

In the street, Raven crossed the road casually and walked towards the apartment block. When he neared the lighted entrance he stopped and knelt down to adjust his shoe-string. From under his slouch hat, he surveyed the doorway thoroughly. He was not satisfied with the empty doorway, so he crossed the street again and passed the block on the opposite side. His caution rewarded him.

A little guy, dressed in black, lounged against the wall in the shadows near the entrance. He kept so still that Raven wouldn't have noticed him at all if he'd come straight into the blinding light of the doorway.

The little guy had his hands deep in his coat pockets, and he watched Raven pass on the other side of the street, indifferently.

Raven went on, crossed the road again and turned down a side street. He turned to his right after a few minutes' walking and approached the rear of the apartment block. This time he kept to the shadows. He hadn't gone far before he spotted another little guy, also dressed in black, lounging near the rear exit.

So it wasn't going to be the easy way. He might have known it. It was a cinch that if Mendetta had guards outside the block, there would be guards inside as well.

Raven went on, his head thrust forward, the line of his jaw fixed, and his thin lips compressed. He knew Mendetta couldn't escape from him. It was just a matter of time.

4

June 5th, 1.40 a.m.

Jay got round to the 22nd Club twenty minutes before it closed down for the night. There were a lot of people dancing and drinking, and he went immediately to the bar.

The bartender looked at him and rang a bell in Grantham's office by pressing his toe on a button on the floor. His well-disciplined face smiled at Jay, and he asked him what he'd like. Jay ordered a beer.

Benny Perminger came up at the moment, very hot and damp, and ordered a double Scotch. He seemed delighted to see Jay.

"What a stranger," he said; "and drinkin' beer too! Don't you know it's bad etiquette to drink beer in a joint like this?"

Jay shook hands with him. "I don't have to worry about such things," he said seriously. "No one expects a newspaper man to behave like a human being. How's the motor trade?"

Benny shook his head. "Lousy," he said. "There's too much competition. Seriously, Jay, I'm havin' a bad time just gettin' along."

Jay pursed his lips. There were always guys who had a bad time getting along, but they went to places like the 22nd Club and spent as much in a night as he earned in a week. Benny was one of these.

"I saw your chief. Poison, the other night. My God! Have you seen his car? It's just a ruin on four wheels. It's time he had a new one."

Jay shrugged. "Poison's old-fashioned. He likes that car. Maybe he's got sentimental memories."

"I don't believe it; he's just mean. Listen, Jay, could you put in a word for me? If I could get that old buzzard to take a trial run I'd hook him, but I can't get near him."

Jay promised to do what he could.

"There's another guy who I want to get in with. That's Mendetta. He could use a flock of my cars. I do trucks now, you know. Beggars can't be choosers. I guess that guy could use a lot of trucks. I've been trying to persuade Grantham to get me an introduction, but he doesn't seem keen. I suppose I'll have to offer him a split in my commission."

"Does Grantham know Mendetta?" Jay asked, suddenly interested.

"Know him? Why, of course he knows him. I thought everyone knew that. Mendetta put up the dough for this Club. He's got his finger in every pie."

Jay drank some beer. "Aaah," he said, putting the glass down, "Mendetta's a bad guy. I'd forget about him."

Benny shrugged. "What the hell. His dough's good, ain't it?" he said. "I don't care who buys my cars as long as he pays."

Jay finished his beer. "Maybe you're right," he said.

Just then a blonde came in, followed by a tall young man with heavy, horn-rimmed glasses. The blonde wore a red dress, very tight across her small breasts, and when she climbed up on the high stool at the bar she showed a lot of her legs.

Benny looked at her. He stared so hard that she giggled suddenly and adjusted her skirt. Benny sighed. "There're an awful lot of swell dames around tonight," he said to Jay. "She's nice, ain't she?"

Jay wasn't very interested. "Sure," he said; "they're all nice. Where's your wife? How is she, anyway?"

Benny still looked at the blonde. "Sadie? Oh, she's fine. She's out there with my party. I sort of wanted a drink. Did I? No, that's wrong. I came out for a doings. Seeing you put it out of my mind. I guess I'd better get on." He shook hands again and went off.

Jay ordered another beer. While he was waiting for it, he saw Grantham come in. Grantham was very tall and thin, with silver-white hair. His face was hard. Two lines ran from his nose to his mouth, and he looked very grey. Jay only knew him by sight, he'd never spoken to him. When he saw him, he turned back to the bar and paid the bartender.

Grantham came up and stood at his elbow. "What do you want?" he said. His voice was very hostile.

Jay looked at him by turning his head. "Should I know you?" he asked. "Are you someone I ought to know?"

Grantham introduced himself. "We don't have newspaper men in here, you know," he said; "we don't like them in here."

Jay raised his eyebrows. "That's interestin'," he said. "That's very interesting. No newspaper men, huh? And who else? Tell me your black list. I bet you don't like the cops in here either."

Grantham tapped a little tune on the counter. "Don't let's get sore about this," he said evenly. "I'm just telling you. Maybe you didn't know."

"Is this your idea, or did Mendetta suggest it?"

Grantham's face hardened. "That sort of talk won't get you anywhere," he said quietly. "I'm just telling you to keep out of here, that's all."

Jay shook his head. "You can't do that. This is a place for public entertainment. I should forget about it. A line or two in my paper could upset your business pretty badly."

Grantham nodded. "I see," he said; "I was just giving you a hint. You don't have to take it. You're quite right, of course. You have every right to come here. Only you're not welcomed."

"Leave me now, pal," Jay said, turning away, "I'm goin' to have a good cry."

Grantham looked at the barman and then at the clock. "You can shut down, Henry," he said, and walked away.

Jay finished his beer, nodded to the barman, who ignored him, and went out into the big lounge. People were beginning to move out. He saw Clem Rogers, who played the saxophone in the band, putting his instrument away. He knew Rogers quite well.

He went to the cloakroom and got his hat, and then he went outside. He had to wait ten minutes before Rogers came out, and then he followed him away from the Club. When they got to the main street he overtook him.

Rogers seemed surprised to see him. "You're late, ain't you?" he said, peering at his wrist-watch. It was just after two o'clock.

Jay fell in step beside him. "We newspaper guys never sleep," he said. "How about a little drink? There's a joint just down here that keeps open all night."

Rogers shook his head. "I guess not," he said. "I want to get home. I'm tired."

Jay put his hand on his arm and steered him down a side turning. "Just a short drink, buddy," he said, "then you can go home."

They went down some steps to an underground bar. The place was nearly empty. A short, thick-set Italian dozed across the bar. He raised his head sleepily as the two entered.

"Good evenin'," he said, rubbing the counter-top with a swab. "What will you have?"

"At this time of night, Scotch," Jay said. "Bring us the bottle over there." He indicated a table at the far end of the room.

Rogers followed him across and sat down. He yawned, rubbing his eyes with his hands. "God! I'm tired," he said. "I wish I could get some other job. This is killin' me."

Jay poured out a big shot of whisky in each glass. "I ain't goin' to keep you long, but there's just one little thing you might help me with."

"Sure, I'd be glad to. What is it?"

"You must see everything that goes on at the Club. I've got a feeling it ain't quite on the level. I want to find out."

Rogers sat back. His sleepy eyes suddenly woke up. "I don't know what you mean," he said.

"Just that. How does the place strike you?"

Rogers blinked. "You tryin' to get the place shut down?" he asked, a little coldly.

Jay hesitated, then he said, "That's about it. Now, look here, Rogers, you know me. I wouldn't make things difficult for you. I know you've got to think of your job, but if you helped me I'd see you all right."

"Yeah? How?"

"How would you like to work for Cliff Somers? I could get you an in with his outfit if you fancied it."

Rogers' face brightened. "Honest?"

Jay nodded.

"I'd like that. I've always wanted to work for Somers. He's got a swell crowd."

"I know, but I'd only get you in if you made it worth while. You've got to tell me things."

Rogers shook his head. "I guess that's too bad," he said. "There's nothin' to tell. The Club's like hundreds of other clubs. Maybe there's a fight now and then between two drunks, but that's nothin'."

Jay pulled a face. "I didn't think there was anything wrong with the joint," he admitted, "but I was hoping you'd know something."

Rogers shook his head. "No, I guess not." He finished his drink.

"Think back," Jay urged him. "Hasn't anythin' happened that made you curious? Anythin' that somebody did or said."

Rogers yawned. "No, I don't think so," he said, staring with sleepy eyes at the bottle of Scotch. "Mind you, there was one violent drunk that made a bad scene a couple of months ago, but that wasn't anythin' really."

Jay shifted impatiently. "Well, tell me."

"There was nothin' to it. Some guy wanted to see Grantham. He wasn't well dressed. Looked like a clerk in an office or somethin'. I thought it was odd that he should come to the Club.

When Grantham didn't show up he started to shout. Some bull about where his sister was or somethin'. We didn't pay much attention to him. They gave him a bum's rush. Treated him pretty roughly. We haven't seen him again."

"What about his sister?"

Rogers shrugged. "Search me. He's lost her or somethin'. Seems to have thought that Grantham knew where she was. I guess he was drunk."

"Did he look drunk?"

"No, now you come to think of it, he didn't, but I guess he must have been. You don't start shouting around a joint like the 22nd unless you're drunk, do you?"

"Still it's rum, ain't it?" Jay turned it over in his mind. "Know who he is?"

Rogers frowned. "I did hear his name. I've forgotten. It wasn't important, you see."

"Think. I want to find that guy. Maybe he knows somethin'."

Rogers tried to concentrate. "It was quite an ordinary name. I tell you what. Gerald Foster, the shipping man, seemed to know him. He was having dinner at the time. When this guy started shouting, he looked round and seemed to recognize him. He got up and told him not to make a fool of himself. You might ask him."

Jay said he would. He stood up. "I ain't keepin' you out of your cot any longer," he said. "Keep your ears open, won't you?"

Rogers got up. "You really meant what you said about Somers?"

"I'll see him tomorrow," Jay promised.

They went out into the street.

"It's mighty dark, ain't it?" Rogers said, groping his way up the stone steps.

Jay followed him. "It's all right when you get used to it," he returned. "Come on, I'll go some of the way home with you."

They parted when they came to the trolley stop. Rogers went off to collect his car from a near-by garage, and Jay waited for a trolley. He was quite satisfied with his evening's enquiries. He didn't expect to find anything but at least he could tell Henry that he was following up an angle that might bring in something. If they could only keep Poison quiet for a week or so, he might simmer down.

He saw the lights of the trolley as it swung round the corner. He'd be glad to get home, he told himself.

5

June 5th, 2.15 a.m.

Raven couldn't sleep. He moved through the dark streets, his sour, bitter hatred refusing to let him rest. He walked automatically, not noticing where he was going. He wanted to vent his vicious hatred on someone who couldn't strike back. He wanted to sink his hands into flesh and rend.

The picture of Mendetta, comfortable in his luxury apartment, carefully guarded, made him sick with jealousy. Mendetta had got to go. Once he was out of the way, the organization would fold up. It was Raven's chance. He could step in then. They were all afraid of him. There might be a little trouble, but not for long. It was Mendetta who held them together. It was Mendetta who was keeping him away from power. Grantham would be easy. He was too fond of the things he already possessed to risk anything. Raven knew that he had only to walk into the 22nd Club to take over when Mendetta was out of the way.

He turned left into the darkness and plodded on, his mind busy with schemes. The muscles in his legs were fluttering, crying out for rest, but his brain was too active. He had been walking a long time, thinking, planning and scheming.

Out of the darkness, someone called to him. The sound of the voice startled him, and he stiffened as he turned his head.

A girl stepped away from the railings of a house and came close to him. He could see the pale blur of her face and the inviting, swaying movement of her body as she came towards him.

She said in a soft, husky voice, "Come home with me, darlin'."

Raven hated her viciously. His first conscious reaction was to smash his fist in her face. He found that he was too tired even to do that. Instead, he moved on, ignoring her.

She took two quick steps and was beside him again. "Come

on," she said urgently, "it's just round the corner. Spend the night with me, honey. I'm good—honest, I wouldn't tell you if I wasn't."

He stopped walking and half turned. It suddenly dawned on him that she must be one of Mendetta's whores. She was in Mendetta's district. A murderous desire suddenly surged through him.

She came very close and put her thin white hand on his sleeve. He couldn't bear her to touch him, and he shook her off savagely.

"What's the matter, honey, ain't you well?" She began to draw back, suddenly uneasy.

He looked up and down the deserted street. No, not here. He'd have to go back to her place. His thin mouth curled into a smile. This would make Mendetta sit up all right. He said, "Well, come on, then. Where do we go?"

At once she became bright again. He felt against his face her little sigh of relief. She said, "Gee! You scared me. I thought you were a cop."

He began to move down the street with her, taking long, shambling, unsteady steps.

As he didn't say anything, she went on, "A girl's gotta look out for herself. It's a tough life, darlin'. You're goin' to give me a nice present?"

Still he didn't say anything. Her voice, her scent and her walk all infuriated him, but she was one of Mendetta's possessions. He mustn't say or do anything that would frighten her until he got her where she couldn't get away. As he didn't trust himself, he kept silent.

He was conscious that she was looking at him closely, and that her step lagged a little. He put his hand on her arm and hurried her along. "Where is it?" he said.

"Here," she said a little breathlessly. "Let me get my key."

He stood back while she searched in her cheap little bag. They were directly under the street light. He could see her brass-coloured hair, her wide rouged mouth, her short nose and her hard, professional eyes. She only came to his shoulder, and under her tight bottle-green dress he could see the outline of her small, firm breasts.

He said harshly, "For God's sake hurry."

She giggled nervously. "I'm hurrying."

He could have spat in her face. She turned and smiled at him. "There's a hole in the lining, I guess," she said.

At the corner of the street, a cop suddenly appeared. Raven saw him instantly. The inside of his mouth went very dry, and he said once again, "Hurry."

The tone of his voice startled her, and something of his urgency infused her with panic. She fumbled with her key, jabbing at the keyhole unsuccessfully.

With an obscene word on his lips, he snatched the key from her fingers and opened the door. He put his hand on her shoulders and shoved her inside, stepping in behind her and closing the door softly. He could feel the cold sweat under his arms.

She said a little angrily, "Why did you do that?"

"Put a light on."

He could hear her fumbling along the wall, and then the passage was swamped with a bright hard light. He said, "Well, go on. Don't stand there."

She hesitated. "I don't know about you. There's something I don't like about you."

He pushed his hat to the back of his head and looked her full in the face. They looked at each other for a long minute.

"Do you always yap like this?" he snarled at her. "Take me to your room."

They went upstairs. He followed her closely. As she went up before him he could see how her hips rolled as she lifted her feet. The professional skirt was so tight across her hips he could see where her suspender belt ended and where the little knobs of the suspenders caught her stockings.

They went up three flights in silence. Then she stopped and opened a door. He caught a glimpse of a little brass plate on the door as he entered a box-like hallway. He closed the door behind him. She took him into the bedroom.

He stood in the middle of the room, his ears intent, listening.

She said, "Come on, darlin'. Don't stand there."

"You alone up here?"

"Sure, we won't be disturbed."

Still he stayed listening. She said again impatiently, "What is it?"

He chewed his lower lip, looking at her thoughtfully, then he said, "Mind if I look?" and went out, throwing open the other doors without entering. He glanced in the other two rooms, satisfying himself that they were empty.

She followed him into the hall. Her face was hard and her eyes glittered angrily. "What the hell do you think you're doin'?" she snapped. "This is your room here. The rest of this joint is private—do you get it?"

Raven again felt like smashing his fist in her face, but he held himself in. "Okay, okay," he said, walking past her into the bedroom.

She shut the other two doors and then followed him in. Once more her lips broke into her professional smile, but her eyes were dark and suspicious. She said, "Come on, darlin'. Let's get it over."

Raven took off his hat and ran his fingers through his short, wiry black hair. He sank on to the bed, which gave under his weight.

The room was shabby and not over-clean. The strip of carpet that lay on the floor was threadbare, and from where he was sitting he could see a small stack of soiled underclothes behind an easy-chair.

While he sat there she took off her dress by just pulling a zipper and stepping out of it. Underneath she wore a pair of pink step-ins and a brassiere. She swayed a little before him, turning this way and that, so he could see her. Then she said, "My present?" Her hard face lighted up with a glittering smile.

Raven put his hand in his pocket and offered her a twenty-dollar bill. It was all the money he had in the world. The amount took her breath away. She clutched at the bill and stood staring at it. "Migod, you're cute!" she said. "Gee! I'll give you a good time for this."

The bill disappeared into the top of her stocking, and she hurriedly stripped down to her suspender-belt. She said, coming round the bed, "Come on, darlin', come on."

He said, "Don't be in such a hurry. Put on a wrap or somethin'. I want to talk to you."

He saw her go a little limp. "Aw, come on, darlin'. We can talk afterwards."

"No."

She hesitated, then, shrugging, crossed the room and took a dark red silk wrap off the door-peg.

Raven, sitting in the chair, looked at her indifferently. He noticed she had a little roll of fat above her hip bones, and he thought her buttocks looked ridiculous framed in the soiled suspender-girdle. A dame had got to be good just wearing a girdle, stockings and shoes. This whore wasn't so hot.

She put the wrap on and wandered over to the bed. "You've got to be quick, darlin'," she said. "I can't keep you here all night."

Raven shook his head. "I shan't stay all night," he said. "Who's underneath?"—pointing to the floor.

"No one. All offices," she said. "I keep telling you no one'll disturb you." Then a thought crossed her mind. "Say, the bulls aren't looking for you, are they?"

A thin smile came to Raven's lips. "Not yet, they ain't," he returned.

There was a long silence. His cold, wolfish face, his hooded eyes, made her very uneasy. She'd kicked around with plenty of toughs and hoods in her time, but this guy was different. She felt suddenly scared of him, and horribly alone. He just sat there, gripping the arms of the chair, watching her indifferently.

She felt a little sick. "Hell!" she thought. "What a dumb thing to have told him I'm alone!"

He said, "You belong to Mendetta's bunch, don't you?"

Her eyes opened very wide. She didn't expect anything like that. "Mendetta? I've never heard of him," she said hastily.

"No?" Raven crossed his leg. "You surprise me. Mendetta runs all this territory, including the whores."

"Don't call me that," she snapped. "If you're goin' to be funny, you better beat it."

"Mendetta's a big shot around here. He runs everything. He makes plenty of dough, but he ain't goin' to last. Do you hear, baby? He ain't goin' to last."

She looked over at the door. "Can't you lay off this crap? I don't know what you're talkin' about. I'm tired. I gotta get some sleep. Let's get this over, an' then you beat it."

Raven nodded. "Don't work yourself into a lather, sister. Get on the bed. We're goin' to get some sleep right now."

She dug up a false smile. "That's fine, darlin'. I don't know anythin' about this Mendetta guy." She went over to the door. Her heart was beating wildly, and she kept her eyes averted so that he shouldn't see her panic.

He said in a chilly voice: "I said get on the bed."

She put her hand on the door-knob. "I'll be right back," she said hurriedly. "I'll be right back."

Before she could open the door, he had left the chair, shoved her away from the door, slammed and locked it. He took the key out of the lock and dropped it into his pocket.

The look on his face terrified her, but she tried to bluff. "Get out of the way an' unlock the door," she said weakly.

He thrust out his hand and sent her sprawling over the bed. He leant against the door. "When I tell you to do a thing—you do it."

She struggled to a sitting position. "Unlock that door, you big bastard," she said. "Get out of here. Go on, take your dough and beat it." She flipped the twenty-dollar bill from the top of her stocking and threw it at him.

Raven bent slowly and picked it up. He walked over to the bed and sat down beside her. She saw the look in his face. She saw he was going to kill her. The blank, set look in his eyes paralysed her. She could only thrust out her arms. "No... don't!" she cried. "You're not to—do you hear?... No!... Keep away...."

He leant slowly towards her. As he came nearer, she crouched away until she lay flat on the bed, his face hovering just above her. She couldn't scream. Her tongue curled to the roof of her mouth and stayed there. She couldn't do anything. Even when his hands slid up to her throat she only clutched feebly at his wrists, shaking her head imploringly at him.

He said softly, "It won't hurt, if you don't struggle."

She shut her eyes, and as the blood began to drum in her ears she suddenly realized that this was death, and she began to fight him frantically. She had left it too late. His knee, driving into the little hollow between her breasts, pinned her like a poor moth to the bed. The vice-like grip of his fingers cut the air from her lungs.

He said, "Mendetta will hear about this. He'll hate it. He'll know then someone is after him. Do you hear, you silly little fool? You couldn't earn enough to live decently. Look at this room. Look at the poverty of it. When I run this territory my broads won't live like this. Do you hear?"

She beat his face with her hands, but she had no strength. Her legs thrashed up and down, at first violently, then jerkily, and then not at all.

As her tongue filled her wide-open mouth, and her eyes tried to burst from their sockets, he turned his head slightly so he couldn't see her. He said in a whisper, "You ugly little bitch." Then blood ran on to his hands from her nose, and she went limp. He climbed off her and stood looking down at her.

He knew that he could go home and sleep now. For a time his hatred had gone out of him.

6

June 5th, 10.15 a.m.

The sun came through the windows of Mendetta's apartment and made patterns on the white carpet.

Remains of breakfast on a silver tray stood on a little table by the settee. An ash-tray gave out a thin grey smoke of a dying cigarette.

Jean, still in a bed-wrap, lay on the settee, her eyes closed and her thoughts far away. She was trying to imagine her life without Mendetta. It was difficult to imagine. It would be difficult also to replace this luxury. But she knew that she couldn't live with Mendetta much longer.

The telephone rang shrilly. It startled her. She reached out and took the receiver off. "Who is it?" she said. Her voice was deep, almost man-like.

Grantham said, "Where's Mendetta?" He sounded very excited.

Jean looked up at the ceiling. She hadn't much use for Grantham. "He's out," she said briefly. "What's wrong?"

"Where is he? I've gotta get in touch with him."

"He's gone round to fix Poison. You can't get him there. What is it? I'll tell him."

There was a pause. "No, I guess I'll wait." Grantham sounded worried.

"Listen, tell me. Maybe I can get hold of him."

"It's one of the girls. She was strangled last night."

Jean's eyes narrowed. "Well, what of it? Tootsie can't do anything about that."

"I know he can't; but he's gotta know."

"All right, I'll tell him. Who did it?"

"The cops don't know."

"I didn't ask that. I said who did it?"

Again there was a long pause. Then Grantham said, "You're not to tell Mendetta this, it'll only make him mad, but I think Raven did it."

Jean sat up. "Why do you say that?"

"One of the patrolmen thought he recognized him going into the girl's apartment. You know, O'Hara. He keeps an eye on that beat. I slipped him a hundred bucks to keep his mouth shut."

Jean thought for a moment. "Raven?" she repeated. "I wonder. Does that mean—?"

"I don't know, but he said he'd start something, didn't he?"

"He said he'd get Tootsie. Listen, what are you going to do if he gets Tootsie?"

"Don't talk like that," Grantham said sharply. "He won't get him. Tootsie's too big. He's too well protected."

"I know, but suppose he does. Raven's dangerous; he might, you know. What will you do?"

"What the hell can I do? I couldn't afford to fight him. He's got quite a big mob, and they're dangerous. At this time, we can't afford a gang battle."

Jean smiled. "You mean you'd let him walk in?"

"What else could I do? The boys only keep together because of Tootsie. If Tootsie went, they'd rat."

"I know."

There was a long silence.

"Listen, Jean, you don't think—?"

"I don't think anything, but you and me've got to look after ourselves, haven't we?"

"Well, yes, I guess that's so, but nothing's going to happen to Tootsie. I know nothing will happen to Tootsie."

Jean smiled again. "I'm glad to hear you say so," she said, and hung up. She lay thinking for a long time, then she picked up the telephone and called a number.

Someone asked roughly what she wanted.

"I want to speak to Raven," she said softly. "Yes, tell him it's Jean Mendetta. Yes, he'll speak to me all right," and she lay back, an amused smile on her mouth, waiting for Raven to come to the phone.

7

June 5th, 11.20 a.m.

Jay took a taxi to the east side of the town. He was feeling pleased with himself. As soon as he had reached the office he had got Gerald Fisher on the phone and asked him about the scene Rogers had told him about.

Fisher remembered it quite well. "What do you want to know about that for?" he asked suspiciously.

"I want to find the guy who made the scene," Jay said. "He might have an important bearing on a big case we're working on now. I don't say he has, but there is just the chance. I was hoping you might help me."

"As a matter of fact, I do know him. He used to be one of my clerks. That was why I was so surprised to see him at the 22nd Club. His name's Fletcher. Do you want his address? I could get it for you."

"Sure, that's just what I do want."

"Just a moment, then." Jay heard Fisher say something, then he came on the line again. "They're looking it up. We've got in on record, I know."

"He doesn't work with you any more?"

"Good God, no! I couldn't have a fellow in my office like that. He made a frightful fool of himself. He had to be tossed out. I gave him the sack next morning."

"What was the trouble, Mr. Fisher?" Jay asked.

"I don't know. He must have been drunk. He kept on yelling about his sister. I mean to say, that sort of thing isn't done at the 22nd. No, I had to get rid of him."

Jay grinned. "Sure," he said.

"Ah, here's the address."

Jay wrote it down, thanked Fisher, and hung up. He

thought maybe he was going on a fool's errand, but it was worth trying, anyhow.

The taxi drew up outside a large tenement house. The driver said apologetically, "This is it, boss."

Jay got out and paid him off. He walked up the steps and rang on the bell. The place was dirty and horribly sordid. He felt people watching him behind ragged curtains all down the street.

An old woman, very dirty, with a sack for an apron, opened the door and looked at him suspiciously.

Jay raised his hat. "Mr. Fletcher in?" he asked.

"He's on the top floor. You can go up." She stood aside to let him in. "You tell that guy to pay his rent. I'm gettin' sick of askin' him myself."

Jay ignored her and went up the stairs. A big negro lounged against the wall on the first landing and looked at him insolently. As Jay passed he spat on the floor.

On the top floor a large fat woman sat just outside her door, peeling potatoes. Jay asked her where Fletcher's room was. She jerked her thumb to a door without saying anything.

Jay rapped on the door and pushed it open.

A man lay on a dirty mattress. He'd got a three days' growth of beard, and Jay saw he was blind in one eye. He sat up, a scared look on his face, as Jay entered.

"What do you want?" he said. He had quite a cultured voice.

Jay looked round the dirty room and grimaced. "I'm Ellinger of the *St. Louis Banner*. I want to talk to you, pal," he said.

Fletcher got off the bed. "I don't want to talk to anyone," he said.

Jay thought he looked horribly thin. He began to cough and he had to sit on the bed again.

Jay pulled up a rickety chair and sat down too. "Listen, Fletcher, don't fly off the handle. You're lookin' in a bad shape. I might be able to help you."

When he had stopped coughing, Fletcher said rather wildly, "Look what they did!"—pointing to his eye. "They did that. Threw me down a flight of stone steps. One of the heels hit me in my eye with his elbow."

Jay lit a cigarette. He didn't like the smell of dirt in the room. "That's what I've come to see you about," he said. "What's it all about? If I can help you I will."

Fletcher looked at him suspiciously. "Why?" he demanded. "Why should you want to help me?"

"Now don't get that way. Been out of a job some time, haven't you? Now come on, spill it."

"It's Janet," Fletcher began. Then suddenly his thin face crumpled and he began to cry.

Jay pushed his hat to the back of his head and blew out his cheeks. He was very embarrassed. "What you want is a drink," he said. "You wait. I'll get you one."

Fletcher controlled himself with an effort. "No, don't go away," he said. "I'm all right. I guess I'm sort of low. I haven't had much grub."

"Well, come on. I'll buy you a lunch." Jay got up. Fletcher shook his head. "Not now. Later, perhaps, but I want to tell you." Jay sat down again. "Go ahead," he said. "It's my sister, Janet. She went away one morning to work and she didn't come back. I've hunted everywhere. I've told the police, but they can't find her."

Jay sighed. He knew there were a lot of girls in St. Louis who went out and didn't come back any more. "Maybe she went off and got married. Maybe she thought she'd like to go to Hollywood. There're a lot of girls who suddenly get a bug in their conks and beat it without telling anyone."

Fletcher looked up. His one eye burnt fiercely. "You don't believe that rubbish, do you?" he said. "That's what the police said."

Jay shifted. "Well, what else could have happened to her? You don't think she's dead, do you?"

"I wish to God she was!" He beat his fist on his knee. "The Slavers have got her!" he shouted. "Do you hear? The Slavers have got her."

"You don't know that. You only think they have. There ain't much of that stuff going on now. We've cleaned it up."

"You're wrong. It's going on every day of the year. Decent girls leaving their homes and being trapped. Decent girls forced into brothels. Any amount of them. And there's nothing done about it. The police know all about it, but they keep their mouths shut. Anyone who gets to know about it is given money to keep his mouth shut."

"You can't talk like that unless you've got some proof. Why

did you kick up that row at the 22nd Club?"

"Can't you guess? Grantham's working the racket."

"You're crazy. Grantham? Don't talk bull."

Fletcher lay back on his elbow. "I've been watching him," he said. "One night, when the Club was closed, I saw a car draw up outside the Club. The street was empty. No one saw me. They took a girl out of the car. She had a rug over her head. Just as she got to the door she got the rug off and she screamed. They hit her on the head with something. They hit her very hard. I could hear the sound very distinctly from where I was standing. Then they carried her inside. You don't think anything of that? Well, I'll tell you some more." There was a crazy gleam in his eye. "Another night I got on the roof. You've never been on the top floor of the Club, have you? Nor have I. But I've been on the roof. I've listened, lying on the tiles with my ear close to the roof, listening. I've heard things. I've heard girls screaming. I've heard the crack of whips. I've heard a lot of horrible things."

Jay was interested now. "You're sure of all this?" he said.

Fletcher leant forward and grabbed his coat lapels. "Do you think I'd make it up? Don't you realize what all this means? My sister was one of those girls. She was taken into that place. They beat her until she was willing to do what they wanted. She's somewhere in this town, selling her body to anyone who'll pay for it. Do you hear? And everyone sits around, blast them, and tells me that it couldn't happen here. That this town's been cleaned up. And it's going on now... now... now!"

Jay pushed him back on to the bed gently. "Take it easy," he said. "I believe you, anyway. Listen, Fletcher, you've got to use your brains. It's no good getting in a state about this. You'll be wanted to give evidence. I'll see that you get some money and I'll fix a job for you. You'll have to leave everything to me. I'm going out after this business. We want to close the Club up, and you've given me the right lever to do it with. Leave it to me. I'll fix those heels."

Later, after he had made arrangements for Fletcher, he took a taxi back to the Banner office. The taxi couldn't drive him fast enough.

8

June 5th, 10.40 p.m.

Benny Perminger just wasn't interested in the fight any more. From the first gong he'd sat forward, his jaw set and thrust out, and his hands clenched on his knees. He'd given them three rounds to get warmed up. These big guys couldn't take chances in the first few rounds. They'd got to get set and take stock of each other, so Benny was patient.

All right, this was the fifth round coming up and nothing had happened. These two punks just seemed to love each other. They poked feebly, and then shuffled into a clinch, then they'd break away, look at each other like they were surprised to see they were still standing up, and then start poking and clinching all over again.

Benny sat back suddenly with a long-drawn-out sigh of disgust. That's when it happened. His ears slid along silk stockings. You don't go getting your head between a dame's knees every day. It shook him up. It took his mind right off the fight and kept it off.

The dame shifted back fast enough, but it didn't alter the fact. Benny had had his head between her knees. She had been sitting right behind him on the tier seat. Maybe, she'd never seen a fight before, so she got excited. She came forward, with her knees hovering over Benny's head.

Benny was sitting forward too. There was nothing in it, both sitting forward trying to squeeze some excitement out of a punk fight. It was different when Benny sat back suddenly. It gave her quite a shock when Benny's head banged between her knees. The way that dame slid back on her seat was nobody's business.

Her boy friend was quick too. One of those guys who missed nothing. He said, "Go on, give it away. Put it on a plate an' hand it round. Don't mind me."

Benny heard him. He sounded tough, so Benny sat still, feeling a little sick. He kept his eyes on the two punks shuffling around on the resin. He stole a quick look at Sadie, sitting beside him, but she hadn't noticed anything. She was half asleep.

Fights bored her, anyway, but she'd got into the habit of going places with Benny. She liked best when they went to movies, because he didn't get excited, or look at other women, or curse.

It was a lucky break for Benny that one of the fighters suddenly thought it was time to go home. He began to hit more seriously and immediately got the other guy in trouble. All the crowd began to shout and get excited, so Benny felt a lot less scared.

All the same, he had lost interest in the fight. He wanted to have a look at this dame behind him. He knew that if he did he'd start something, so he just stared down at the brightly lit ring and made up pictures of what she might look like.

It wasn't long before he'd got such a picture that he could hardly sit still. There were two more fights on the programme, but they weren't going to keep Benny sitting in that hall. He wanted to get home with Sadie, just as fast as his car would take him.He said, "Come on, honey, let's get outta here."

Sadie woke up and blinked around, stared at the two little men way down in the ring, and then looked blankly at Benny. "Where's the fire?" she said.

Benny looked at her. She was good. She was just the right height, and her hair was curly, black and silky. She reminded Benny of the cuties who give you thoughts from the front cover of College Life. They'd been married now two years, and Benny liked her a lot. He had even kept off other girls. Sadie had been pretty good to him. The first six months had gone well for them both.

Then Benny got used to it, and he began to slip back.

At first he'd walk along with Sadie and compare her with other dames. Sadie was good, so she came out well in that game. When he began wondering what the other dames were like, then that wasn't so good. He knew what Sadie was like. Then, from just looking, he had to make remarks. He'd say to Sadie, "Did you see that dame, just then? Gee! What a figure! Did you see anythin' like that?"

Well, Sadie felt pretty safe, and she thought Benny was just kidding her, but Benny wouldn't leave it alone. He'd say, "I bet that dame's a hot one. Yeah, look at the way she swings her can. Gee! I guess that dame gets pushed around plenty."

Nothing in it, but it hurt. It did more than that, it got on Sadie's nerves. She knew that one of these days he was going to cheat. Once he'd started cheating he'd go on cheating. It was no good. She'd done everything she could to hold him, but he'd got that sort of a mind. He couldn't help himself.

When he went and put his head between that flossie's knees, something snapped inside Sadie. That finished it. He didn't think she'd seen that. All right, it'd be a surprise for him.

Benny said again, "Come on, honey. Those punks'll drive me crazy."

They pushed their way past the other people and got to the gangway. Benny looked back. Sadie was waiting for him to do that. Benny's heart jumped when he saw the dame. Boy! She was good. It made him go limp inside just to think that he'd slid his ears along her stockings.

Sadie said it for him. "I know," she said; "don't tell me. She's cute. She's got everything. She's a menace to good men, and she's the world's biggest push-over."

Benny blinked at her. "Hey! Where do you get that stuff?"

Sadie walked down the gangway, not listening to him. She was conscious of some of the men drawing their eyes reluctantly from the fight to watch her go. She swung her hips. "Go on," she thought, "take a look at me. I'm not so bad myself."

Benny came running after her. "What was that stuff about the dame?" he said angrily. "I don't like that line."

Sadie looked at him over her shoulder. "Looked to me like you were having a good time," she said, without stopping.

Benny nearly fell over. She'd seen after all. Hell! He might have guessed that she couldn't have missed that.

He had almost to run to keep up with her. "You ain't mad about a little thing like that?" he said anxiously. "It was an accident—you know that."

She said bitterly, "Sure it was an accident. Pretty nice for you, wasn't it?"

They got to the car, and she beat him to opening the door. She climbed in and sat close up to the door, away from him. He started the engine and began to drive slowly down the winding exit.

"Forget it, baby," he said. "It was just one of those things. Anyway, she wasn't so hot."

Sadie knew he was lying, but she suddenly felt very tired, and she leant back, shutting her eyes.

As she didn't say anything, Benny hopefully assumed she wasn't mad any more. He drove along, his mind half on the traffic, thinking of the dame. She'd been a smasher. To think that had happened. If Sadie hadn't been there, and if that tough hadn't been there, maybe he could have dated her up. It would have been a pushover. It was a natural. He could hardly wait to get the car away.

Sadie leant limply against the wall of the little elevator as it droned up to the sixth floor. She didn't look at him. Benny stood close to her, watching her anxiously as he wiped his sweating hands with a handkerchief. She was looking tired and a little irritable, he thought. Anyway, if he went about it in the right way it'd be all right.

In the early days of marriage he would come in from work, sweep her off her feet into the bedroom, leaving the supper to burn. She'd always protested, but he knew she was pleased as he was when it was over.

The elevator stopped at the sixth floor, and Sadie walked out. On the opposite passage Tootsie Mendetta had his apartment.

It always made Benny mad to think that a rich guy like Mendetta should live just across his passage, and he'd never set eyes on him. He knew he was there, but he'd never seen him. Anyway, right at this minute, he didn't give Mendetta a thought.

He fumbled at the keyhole, making two attempts before he sank the key. His hands shook a little.

Inside the small apartment he let her take off her hat and coat, and then he sidled up behind her. He put his arms round her from behind. "I love you, honey," he said, his voice shaking.

"Put me down!" There was a snap in her voice that jolted him. He put her down and turned her. The cold, hostile look she gave him brought him up short, just like he'd rammed his face against a brick wall.

"Say, what's wrong? I got to thinkin' of you in the car. I thought—I thought maybe we could go back a couple of years."

She said, "Think again."

"What the hell is this?" he said, his disappointment making him suddenly mad with her.

She walked back into the sitting-room. He saw her put her hand to her eyes.

He wandered after her, feeling a suppressed rage welling up in him. He leant against the door-post. "What is it?" he asked.

She said, "You know what it is." Her voice sounded full of tears.

"Don't talk in riddles. If you've got anythin' to beef about, why not save it? Listen, honey," Benny said urgently, "this ain't the time to start fightin'. Come on with me. We'll have a good time together—how's that? You'll feel fine—"

She said, interrupting him: "Wait a minute. You've got a one-track mind. That floosie's got you burnt up, and you think you can take it out of me. 'Pretty-daughter-sitting-on-father's-knee-makes-it-hard-for-mother' complex. Not this mother, it doesn't."

Benny took off his hat and threw it across the room. He was mad. "What the hell's come over you?" he demanded, his voice rising.

Sadie went over and sat on the sofa. "I'm sick of the way you look at women. I've stood as much of it as I'm going to stand. Every woman who walks past you, you must look at. You're not content with just looking. You must tell me. All right, if you want every dame in the street, go and have her, but I shan't be around."

Benny rubbed his nose. "So that's it, is it?" he said, suddenly very quiet. "You're jealous, that's what you are. Listen, I haven't put my hands on one single dame since I married you. Why shouldn't I look at 'em? What's the harm in it, anyway? I'm not doin' anythin' wrong, just looking, am I?"

"That's the way you look at it. I can't do a thing about it. So I've got to walk along the street with you and watch you gape at every girl for the rest of my life, have I?"

Benny sat in a chair opposite her. With a great effort he tried to control his patience. In a patronizing tone he said: "Now, don't be screwy, honey. This is just crazy talk. You're feeling low. Tomorrow, we'll laugh about this. Get all these ideas out of your head and you'll have everything."

"No, I won't."

"You'll have everything."

"No, I won't."

"Now, don't go on like that. I said you'll have everything, and I mean you'll have everything."

Sadie sat up stiffly. "Shall I tell you what? When I said I won't, I mean I shan't have what I want. I'll have what you give me."

Benny felt the blood mounting to his face. "Okay, if that's the way you feel. You'll have what I give you—so what?"

"Nothing. It's going on the same way as it's been going on for the last six months. Do you know what that is?"

"All right. You tell me."

"I'll be here cooking your food every damn day of the week. I'll be washing out your clothes when they want washing out, which is mighty often. We'll be living in this great apartment, without any servant, so that you can impress your friends. We'll be wondering every day how we are going to meet all the bills. I'll be getting into bed with you and waiting to see if you're too drunk, or if you're too tired. Then I'll be lying awake half the night wondering if anything's gone wrong while you're sleeping. Then I'll be so woke up that I shan't ever get to sleep until it's time to get your food again. That's what."

Benny said between his teeth, "Would you do something for me? Somethin' for me right now?"

Sadie looked at him. "Go on," she said.

"Will you shut up? Will you shut up before you say something that nothin' you'll ever say after can make any difference?"

She shook her head. "No," she said, "I guess not. I guess I'm finished with that stuff. I'm going on talking until I've said my piece. I've waited long enough."

Benny reached for a cigarette. He lit it, noting that his hands shook a little.

Sadie hugged her knees, looking over the top of them at him.

There was a long pause, then she went on: "I've kidded myself until I just can't kid myself any longer. I thought you were a great guy, Benny, honest I did. I thought the world of you. It's not your fault, it's just that I've been kidding myself. You're not a great guy. You'll never be a great guy. You've got something that's stopping you. You want things. You work hard for them, and then you throw them away. You haven't got any feeling for something you've won, only for something you're winning. You got me. I know you didn't have to work hard. I met you halfway. I wanted you too. But I wanted you in a way that you didn't understand. I wanted you to keep. I wanted you in the morning as well as at night. I wanted to go places with you. I wanted you to eat with, to talk with, and to laugh with; but not you, Benny. You didn't want that."

Benny said between his teeth, "I think you'd better stop."

But she went on, as if he hadn't spoken. "Do you think it's fun for me to hear all about the other dames? Don't I keep myself nice? At first, it hurt. Then I got thinking, wondering why I couldn't hold you. I looked at myself. I gave you everything I had. I even did things you wanted me to because I thought you'd be satisfied, but you weren't. When you wanted me, I got to wondering if you were using me and thinking of some other woman you'd seen in the street on the way home. All women are alike in the dark, aren't they, Benny? Well, I'm sick of it. I'm not doing it any more. Go out and have them, Benny, go out and have them."

Benny said, "Have you finished?"

She shrugged. "Don't get mad. It doesn't do any good. Let's face it. One day you'll want to make a move. One day when I'm not nice any more. Then you'll make a move. You won't just look and talk, you'll sneak off and do things. I'm not waiting for that, Benny. I want the break to come now, not when I can't fight it."

Benny got slowly to his feet. "Well, you've had your say, an' I hope you liked it. I'm through. From now on we'll follow our own set of rails. I hope you'll like it. Maybe, after you've done some work, you'll be glad to come back. Anyway, go and try. I'm spending the night somewhere else." He picked up his hat and without looking back, he went out, shutting the door violently behind him.

Sadie sat very still for some time, then she began to cry.

9

June 5th, midnight.

Mendetta nodded to the guard as he passed into the

hallway. It gave him a sense of power and security to have guards patrolling the building all night. Not that he took Raven seriously. He didn't. He regarded Raven as a small-town gangster with a trigger itch. The idea that Raven even had the nerve to threaten him made him laugh. All the same, he took precautions, but it was seldom during the day he remembered that Raven had promised to get him.

He took the elevator to the sixth floor and walked heavily to his apartment. He let himself in and was surprised to find the place in darkness. For a moment he hesitated, and his hand groped for a gun he no longer carried. Then he swore softly and turned on the light.

The room was empty.

He walked over to the settee and took off his hat and light dust-coat. He felt annoyed with himself for being momentarily scared. It was a long time ago since he carried a gun. The time when he had been Legs Diamond's bodyguard. A lot of water had gone under the bridge since then. Now he paid other guys to carry guns for him.

He was also irritated that Jean wasn't in. He felt like amusing himself with Jean tonight. He wondered where the hell she had got to. Wandering into each empty room in turn and not finding her, he turned to the living-room, sulkily. He'd got to ring Grantham, anyway. By the time he was through she'd turn up.

He sat down by the telephone and dialled Grantham's number.

Grantham came on the line almost immediately.

"Well, I fixed it," Mendetta told him. "There ain't goin' to be any trouble."

"No? Well, I'm mighty glad to hear it. Ellinger was in last night, snooping around. I got one of my boys to look after him. He went out with Rogers; then this morning he went round to that screwy little punk Fletcher. Do you remember him?"

Mendetta was faintly bored with all this. "No," he said, "I don't, but it doesn't matter. I'm telling you—"

"Listen, Tootsie, it does matter," Grantham broke in. "Fletcher was the guy who caused that spot of trouble at the Club a while back about his sister."

Mendetta's hard eyes narrowed. "I thought you got rid of that guy," he said angrily. "You say Ellinger's been to see him?"

"Yes."

"Well, what about it?"

"Nothing. I thought I'd tell you."

"You thought you'd tell me!" Mendetta sneered. "Don't you ever use your head? Must I tell you what to do?"

There was a pause, then Grantham said, "Okay, I'll see to it. Poison's fixed, is he?"

"You've got to get rid of Hamsley. Poison didn't know I was interested in the Club. I've got one or two things on Poison." Mendetta smiled into the black mouthpiece.

"Suppose Fletcher told Ellinger something?"

"What if he did? Ellinger's working for Poison, ain't he? Poison will tell him to lay off. I've fixed that."

"Are you sure it's all right?" Grantham insisted anxiously.

"Of course I'm sure. Now forget it, but see that Fletcher is looked after. That guy's been around too long now."

"I'll fix him," Grantham said viciously, and hung up.

Mendetta glanced over at the clock. It was twelve-fifteen. Where the hell was Jean? He got up and took off his coat, going into the bedroom for his silk dressing-gown. When he had fastened the cord about his thick middle he went back to the living-room and fixed himself a drink. He didn't know why, but he felt uneasy and restless.

Wandering over to the card-table, he picked up the deck of cards and shuffled them slowly. His mind wasn't on patience. He stood there, brooding, letting the cards slide through his fingers. He became aware that he was listening intently for any unusual sound. He could hear the faint whine of the elevator and the click of the grille as it moved between floors. The sharp sound of a car hooter and the steady beat of traffic outside suddenly became real to him instead of a background of unconscious noise.

"What the hell's the matter with me tonight?" he growled irritably, throwing down the pack of cards. He walked over to the window and threw it wide open.

The night was hot and still. The full moon, floating just above the distant roof-tops, flooded the street below with a silvery light. He stood watching the traffic for several minutes, letting the hot air fan his face. Then, just as he was about to return to the room, he paused. He leant far forward, looking into the street. His eyes tried to probe the shadows. Except for an occasional car the street was deserted. The guard, who should have been standing by the entrance, was no longer there. Mendetta couldn't believe his eyes. For three months now the guard had stood there, his hand on his gun, watching those who entered the block of apartments. No one could go in who roused his suspicions. For three months Mendetta could look down on him, and smile to himself, confident in his safety. This came as a great shock to him.

He turned back to the room hurriedly. His first thought was to ring Grantham and tell him to send one of the mob over fast to investigate, then he hesitated. It wouldn't do for Grantham to think that he was getting soft. He tried to remember if he had a gun in the place. It was such a long time since he had had a gun. Maybe Jean had one.

He crushed down the little panic that was beginning to form in his brain. This wouldn't do, he thought angrily; the guy down there maybe was standing inside the hall where he couldn't see him. The best thing would be to ring down to the hall porter and find out.

As he went over to the house phone he heard a key turn in the front-door lock. He stiffened, and stood waiting. He was furious with himself to find that his mouth had gone very dry.

The door opened and Jean came in. She was wearing a smartly cut black two-piece suit. She came in slowly, as if she were tired.

Her presence reassured Mendetta, who said angrily, "Where the devil have you been?"

Jean didn't say anything. She stood looking at him, her eyes very scared, and her face thin and bony.

Mendetta repeated, "Where have you been? Did you know the guard ain't on the door? Was he there when you came up?"

Jean shook her head. "No."

"Well, where is he? What's all this about? You look as if you were expecting someone to die."

She looked at him in horror. "Don't say that," she said fearfully.

He took a quick step towards her, but she got out of his way and half ran round the settee. He stood very still, staring at her. "Well, tell me," he said between his teeth, "where have you been?"

She said, "I—ran into an old pal of yours. He insisted on—seeing you." She waved her hand towards the door.

Mendetta turned his head slowly. A cold chill ran down his back. Raven stood in the doorway, his cold face expressionless. A limp cigarette dangled from the side of his mouth, and in his right hand he held a long-barrelled gun.

Mendetta shivered with the shock. His big white hands fluttered, imploring Raven to go away. "What do you want?" he whispered.

Raven jerked the gun. "Sit down, Tootsie," he said, "we got things to talk about."

Mendetta sat by the card-table. He folded his twitching hands on the green cloth. From where he sat he could see Jean, kneeling on the floor. She had covered her head with her arms. Her attitude reminded Mendetta of a woman who is witnessing an unavoidable head-on collision, and turns away in horror before the crash. He suddenly felt very sick.

Raven continued to lean against the doorway. "It's taken time to get around to you, Tootsie," he said, "but I've done it. I said I'd do it, didn't I?" He jerked his head to Jean. "She ratted on you, Tootsie. Don't trust women, they always let you down. She got the guard to go away. She let me up here, just because she was tired of sleeping with you."

Mendetta's face twitched, but he didn't say anything. Jean got suddenly to her feet and ran into the bedroom, shutting the door violently behind her.

Raven shrugged. "She thinks I'm goin' to look after her. You don't have to worry about that. I don't trust her, an' I wouldn't want anythin' you've had your hands on. No, I guess she'll be sorry for what she's done."

Mendetta said in a whisper, "You want this territory, don't you, Raven? Well, you can have it; I'm through."

Raven nodded. "Yeah, you're through all right."

"Listen, let me get out of town. I'll sign it all over to you. You wouldn't want to kill me if I gave it all over to you?"

Raven shook his head. "I don't want to kill anyone. Why should I?"

Mendetta searched the cold face to try to find some comfort for himself there. He could read nothing in the cold, blank eyes.

"I'll sign anythin'," he said eagerly. "What do you want?"

Raven pointed to a pad of paper on the table. "Just write saying that you're giving me your share of the Club. That's all I'll need. Grantham won't make any trouble."

Mendetta hesitated. "I can go if I do that?" he said. "You'll let me leave the town?"

Raven looked at him. "Why should I want to stop you?" he asked.

The two men looked at each other. Mendetta, fat, well dressed, but terrified; and Raven, cold, thin and shabby.

Raven said, "I can't stay here all night."

Already Mendetta's brain was formulating a scheme. His signature on a bit of paper would mean nothing. He would give the signal as soon as Raven had left to have him killed. My God! He'd been a fool not to have got rid of him before. He reached out and pulled the pad towards him. With a hand that no longer trembled he wrote, handing his share of the 22nd Club over to Raven. He signed it with a flourish.

"Give me until tomorrow," he said, throwing the pad across the table. "I'll get out by tomorrow."

Raven stretched out his hand and took the pad; he glanced at the writing and then put the pad in his pocket.

"You don't have to go, Tootsie," he said quietly. "You'll be better off here."

Mendetta suddenly went cold. He got slowly to his feet. "Listen, Raven," he said feverishly, "this is on the level. I've done what you wanted—" He broke off as he saw the vicious gleam in Raven's eye. With a whimper of terror, Mendetta turned and ran blindly across the room and began to pound on Jean's door. "Don't let him kill me... Jean! Stop him! Stop him! Jean, you wouldn't let him kill—"

Moving softly, Raven stepped behind him and shot him through the head. The gun only made a little hissing sound.

Mendetta was opening the door as he fell. The door swung open violently and he sprawled into the room. Jean crouched against the wall and screamed.

Raven looked at her and raised his gun. She saw the little black hole of the barrel pointing at her, and she hid her face in her hands. The heavy .45 bullet smashed two of her fingers before it blew the top of her head off. She fell first on her knees with a thud that shook the room, and then straightened out, her head hitting the carpet with another muffled thud.

Across the passage, Sadie sat up in bed. She thought she had heard a scream in her sleep, but she knew that she had heard the sound of someone falling.

She listened intently, suddenly wishing Benny was by her side. She could hear nothing, but the scream was so real that she got out of bed and hurriedly put on a wrap. She went out of the bedroom into the little hallway. It was all very dark and silent. Putting on the hall light, she went to the front door and raised the letter-box flap. She could see Mendetta's front door, and the gleam of light coming from under it. Seeing the light warned her that she too was showing light, and she turned off the switch, then she resumed her watch on the opposite door.

She was conscious of her heart beating rapidly, and she felt frightened and alone. A presentiment told her that something was going on in Mendetta's apartment, and she stayed there watching for some time. Then, just when she had decided that she had made a mistake, she saw the door opposite opening silently.

Raven stepped out, a bundle of papers under his arm, and his long-barrelled gun in his hand. He looked up and down the passage and then, shutting the apartment door softly, walked swiftly away.

His ruthless look and his gun scared Sadie badly. She lowered the flap softly and ran into her bedroom. She dived into bed and hurriedly pulled up the sheet. She lay shivering, seeing Raven's cold, wolfish face, and wishing that Benny would come back to her.

10

June 5th, midnight.

Jay pushed open Henry's door and strode in. Henry was just going home. He was putting on his hat and admiring himself in the mirror. He looked over his shoulder and scowled at Jay.

"No more tonight," he said firmly. "Look at the time. I ought to have been home hours ago."

Jay sat down in the arm-chair and lit a cigarette. "I got something to tell you," he said; "you'll be interested."

"Yeah? Well, I've got something to tell you. You can forget about the 22nd Club. Poison's just been through."

Jay shook his head. "Oh no," he said. "I've got somethin' on that Club that's goin' to make headlines."

Henry looked at him keenly. "What is it?" he said.

"Grantham's mixed up in a Slave Ring. He uses the Club for immoral purposes."

"You're crazy. Where did you get that stuff?"

Jay grinned. "That's what I thought," he said. "But I've got a guy who's seen and heard things. I'm inclined to believe him. The place wants watching, and maybe we'll find somethin' out."

Henry sat down. "Poison told me to lay off the Club. He's seen Mendetta and they've had a little talk. Mendetta's got an interest in the Club, so Poison doesn't want to do or say anything to upset him."

Jay sneered. "Maybe Poison doesn't know about this Slave angle. It'll make a grand story."

Henry hesitated and then he reached out for the phone. "Shall I see what he says?"

Jay hesitated, then he shook his head. "Will you come with me and meet this guy first? Once you've had a talk with him you'll understand why I'm interested."

"What, now?" Henry demanded. "I can't come now."

Jay got to his feet. "What's the matter with you, Chief? This is goin' to be a big story. We're right in it on the ground floor. I've been waiting a chance to pin somethin' on Mendetta for the last two years. Slavin' is a fine club to beat that heel with. Come on, let's go."

Henry followed him into the elevator. "You're goin' to get somewhere one of these days, Ellinger," he said. "I don't know where, but you'll get there all right."

Jay grinned. "I ain't sentimental, but that guy certainly made me think when he talked about his sister. You gotta daughter, ain't you? I've seen her; she's cute."

Henry looked at him from under the brim of his hat. "What's my daughter got to do with it?"

They walked out of the elevator and crossed the big lobby.

"That's just it, Chief. You guys with daughters don't think about the girls who disappear every year. Let me tell you, if I had a daughter I'd never take my eyes off her. I hope I don't have one."

They got in a taxi and Ellinger gave Fletcher's address.

"What are you talking about?" Henry demanded. "What girls disappearing?"

Jay looked at him. "You know as well as I do. We can't do anythin' about it so we just say they've gone off to get married, or gone to Hollywood or some other excuse. This guy Fletcher is pretty sure that his sister's been slaved. He thinks Grantham, and that means Mendetta too, is trading women. We know there's no proof of it, but, by heavens, think what a stink we could make if we got the proof."

Henry lit a cigar. "All right," he said, "let's see how this guy strikes me. If I think there's anything to it you can go ahead, but Poison will have to give his okay first."

"Poison will okay it if we can convince him. That's why I've got you to come down now. If you think it's all right we'll both go an' see Poison and give it to him with both barrels."

The taxi drove up outside the tenement block. There was a large crowd standing around the front door. An ambulance and two police cars were parked on the opposite side of the street.

Jay bundled out of the car. He looked quickly at Henry, and together they ran up the steps. A big cop stepped in their way. "Take it easy," he said, "you can't come in here."

Jay said, "We're goin' in, buddy. Meet the Editor-in-Chief of the *St. Louis Banner.* Big stuff, boy. Where's your red carpet?"

The cop didn't move. "Yeah?" he said. "If that old guy's the Chief of anythin', then I'm the mother of kittens."

Jay looked at Henry. "He's got you there, Chief," he said with a grin.

Henry said with cold dignity, "What's going on in here?"

Two plain-clothes men from the Homicide Bureau came down the stairs and made to pass them. Henry knew one of them. "Hey, Bradley, tell this flat-foot who I am. I want to go up!"

Bradley looked at him keenly. "For Pete's sake, it's Henry! What are you doin' here?"

Henry smiled easily. "I was passin', saw the ambulance, and thought I'd see my man work first hand."

Bradley shook his head. "It ain't much," he said regretfully; "just another shootin'. Still, you can go on up."

Jay said, "Who is it?"

"Guy named Fletcher. I guess someone owed him a grudge."

Jay shook his head. "I guess we won't bother," he said grimly. "Come on, Chief, that's small-town stuff."

They returned to the taxi, and Jay told the driver to go back to the Banner office.

"Does that interest you?" he said quietly. "Grantham must have found out he'd talked to me, so he shut his mouth. This looks like the real thing."

Henry said doubtfully, "Maybe it was a coincidence."

"Maybe it was nothing of the sort. It sticks out a mile. Who'd want to shoot a guy like Fletcher? Ask yourself. He was just an out-of-work clerk. No, guys don't risk killing a poor punk like that unless it's very important. I'd like you to speak to Poison."

Henry said, "What are you thinking of doing?"

"I'd like to take this up on the quiet. Keep an eye on the Club, find out what I can, and if I get anything worth while, go for it with two hands."

Henry relaxed. "Yeah," he said, "I'll speak to Poison."

"Let's go an' see him now," Jay said. "The old buzzard won't be in bed yet."

Henry groaned. "All right," he said. "It looks as if I'm not going to get any sleep tonight."

"You'll get all the sleep you want after you've seen Poison," Jay said, giving the new address to the taxi-driver.

They had to wait nearly half an hour before Poison would see them. Then he walked into the small reception-room, a heavy scowl on his face and his hands thrust deeply in his trouser pockets.

Poison looked what he was: a millionaire newspaper owner. Hard as nails, a terrific worker, and greedy for dollars. He stared at Henry as if he couldn't believe his eyes. "What do you want?" he snapped. "What is this?"

Henry said respectfully, "This is Ellinger, who's responsible for crime news. He's got a little story that I thought would interest you."

Poison didn't even bother to look at Jay. He tapped Henry

on his chest with a long bony forefinger. "Listen, I pay you to listen to interesting stories, and to print them. I'm far too busy to bother with things like that. Go back to the office, hear his story; if it's any good, print it, if it isn't, tell him to go to hell."

"This story's about Mendetta and the 22nd Club," Henry said patiently. "In view of what you said to me this morning, I thought I'd ask you first."

Poison's eyes snapped. "I said leave the 22nd Club alone. Leave Mendetta alone. When I say a thing I mean what I say."

Henry stepped back. "Very well, Mr. Poison," he said.

Jay said, "Mendetta's running a vice ring. He's trading in women. Decent girls are being kidnapped from their homes. I've got proof that he is using the Club for this purpose. I want your permission to make an investigation."

Poison stiffened. His thin hatchet face went white with anger. Without looking at Ellinger, he said to Henry: "I will not discuss this further. I've told you our policy. Leave Mendetta alone, and leave the Club alone. If any of your staff disobey our policy, get rid of them. Good night." He turned on his heel and walked stiffly out of the room.

Henry looked at Jay. "You heard him," he said.

"I wonder how much Mendetta gave him, the dirty rat-faced heel," Jay said, picking up his hat. "If he thinks he can stop me he's made a big mistake."

Henry looked worried. "You've got to leave it alone, Jay," he said. "Poison's the big shot."

"Yeah? Well, I don't spell it that way," and Jay slammed out of the house.

11

June 6th, 12.30 a.m.

Grantham sat behind his neat desk, writing. A cigarette burnt lazily in an ash-tray at his elbow, and the room was silent but for the faint scratch of his pen.

He heard his door open, and he glanced up irritably. Raven stood looking at him. Behind Raven, Grantham could see Lu Eller, white-faced and uncertain.

Grantham laid down his pen very slowly. The colour went out of his face and a muscle in his jaw began to jump.

Raven said, "Tell this monkey to go away."

Grantham knew that Mendetta was dead. Raven would never have come if Mendetta wasn't dead. He told Eller with his eyes to go away. He didn't trust his voice.

Lu Eller lifted his shoulders. He seemed relieved that Grantham didn't want him. Raven came in and shut the door. He put a slip of paper on Grantham's desk silently.

Without touching it, Grantham read it. It was in Mendetta's handwriting.

"Is he dead?" Grantham said. His voice was very low.

Raven sat down and looked round the office. "He had a little accident," he said. "Things'll be very different now."

"What are you going to do?" Grantham studied the shabby figure sitting before him.

Raven settled back in his chair. "Plenty," he said. "This town was too small for Mendetta and me. One of us had to go. Now I'm takin' it over."

Grantham licked his dry lips. "Mendetta had plenty of protection," he said. "You won't get far without that."

Raven inclined his head. "I've thought of that," he said softly. "That's where you come in. You're going to be my front, Grantham. I've got it all worked out. I'll tell you what to do an' you'll do it. You've done the same thing for Mendetta, so you can do it for me. The difference is that I'm goin' to make more money than Mendetta ever did, an' you're goin' to do a lot more work."

Grantham didn't say anything.

"Don't think you can get out of it. I haven't the time to play around with guys. If you don't like it you'll run into an accident too. Get it?"

"I'll do it," Grantham said quickly. "I've been waiting for you to take over. I knew Mendetta wouldn't last."

Raven inclined his head. "Yeah? You're a smart boy. Okay, tomorrow you an' me'll have a little talk. I want all the dope. I want the names of all the girls who worked for Mendetta. Listen, that guy didn't know how to organize vice. Well, I do. Ever been to Reno, Grantham? No? Well, I have. They make a lot of dough in that town. They understand vice. Well, I've got some ideas. We'll get together." He stood up. "Just so that you don't feel worried about all this, there's a ten per cent cut coming to you on everything if you play ball. If you don't, you'll get a bullet. Think about it."

He wandered to the door.

"I'll be down tomorrow at ten. Get all the stuff together," and he went out, shutting the door softly.

Grantham sat back, feeling slightly sick. So it had happened. Where was Jean? He picked up the phone and hastily dialled Mendetta's number. The operator told him after a short delay that no one was answering. He hung up.

Lu Eller came in. Ever since Mendetta could afford gunmen, Eller had been looking after them. He was a tall, powerfully built man, with a heavy jaw and ingrowing eyebrows.

"What's he want?" he said, standing just inside the doorway.

Grantham lit another cigarette. "That's your new boss," he said bitterly. "Mendetta's met with an accident."

Lu raised his eyebrows. "That's too bad. You standin' for Raven?"

Grantham put his elbows on the table. "Let's face it, Lu," he said. "Since Raven moved in, what's happened? Mendetta lost his grip. We know that. They both came from Chi. Mendetta used to carry a gun for Diamond. He thought he was too big for that, so he moved over here. Well, he got on. What Raven did in Chi. I don't know, but when he came here he certainly scared Mendetta. He offered to come in as a partner, but Mendetta turned him down. You've seen him, haven't you? Looks like he's down to rock bottom, till you look at his face. That guy's going to be big, and Mendetta knew it. When he turned Raven down he signed his death warrant. Raven promised him he'd fix him, and he has. I think Raven can make me more money than any guy in this town. I ain't interested in anything else but making a lot of dough. Raven's good enough for me."

Lu looked at him admiringly. "That's the swellest bit of lyin' I've ever heard. It nearly convinces me, but not quite. Shall I tell you why you're saying welcome to Raven? Because you're yellow. Because Raven's a killer, and you know it. Because Raven's got a little mob that is as tough as hell and could smash us up in half an hour. Yeah, that's why."

Grantham got to his feet. "What about you?" he said. "You

goin' to tell Raven where he gets off?"

Lu shook his head. "Sure I'm not," he said, shrugging his shoulders. "What's good enough for you suits me. I'm yellow too."

"Instead of yapping like this, suppose you go over to Mendetta's apartment and find out what's happened. I'm worried about Jean."

Lu shook his head. "Be your age. Suppose the cops walk in when I'm there? Where should I be? You'll have to wait. The papers'll have it fast enough."

Grantham said uneasily, "Do you think he's killed her too?"

"Why should you worry? She ain't anybody. If you want to know so badly, go an' see for yourself."

Grantham paced up and down the room. "We've got to find out, Lu. This is serious. Suppose Jean talked?"

"She won't talk."

"She might about Raven. If Raven gets pinched, where should we be?"

Lu considered this. "Maybe you're right. Say, isn't O'Hara on that beat?"

"I don't know. Is he?"

Lu turned to the door. "I'll go down there and see. If he is I'll tip him to go up and investigate. What the hell are we payin' that guy two hundred bucks a month for if he can't do a little thing like that?"

Grantham looked relieved. "That's an idea. Get after him right away." Lu left the room at a run.

12

June 6th, 1.10 a.m.

Sadie had just fallen into a light doze when a sound outside her apartment made her sit up, wide awake again.

She listened, her heart beating wildly, the memory of Raven horribly clear-cut in her mind. She wondered if he had returned. For several minutes she lay listening, then, cautiously, she pulled back the bed-clothes and reached for her wrap.

Silently she went to the front door and looked once through

the letter-box. The burly figure of a police officer relieved her of all her fears. He was just going into Mendetta's apartment. She opened the door and stood waiting.

The police officer came out of the apartment in a few minutes. His start of surprise when he saw Sadie puzzled her.

"Is—is anythin' wrong in there?" she asked.

He looked at her suspiciously. "Who are you?" he snapped.

"I'm Mrs. Perminger. I thought I heard someone cry out a little while back and I thought I heard someone fall." Sadie looked at him with big eyes.

O'Hara could have killed her. He'd gone up on Lu's instructions just to look around. He had no intention of reporting Mendetta's death. He had no reasonable excuse for being up there, and now this dame must come and put her oar in.

He said, "I'll come in your place for a moment, Miss. Don't want to be seen in the passage; might scare the folks."

Sadie coloured. "I don't think you'd better come in. I'm—I'm all alone."

O'Hara nodded. "That's all right," he said; "if you'll just let me stand in the hall." He was most anxious that nobody else should see him.

Reluctantly Sadie stepped back and let him in.

"Now then, Miss," he said, taking out his note-book. "You say you heard someone cry out?"

Sadie nodded. There was something about this cop that she didn't like. She wished he'd go away.

"What time was that?"

"It was just after twelve."

"Did you see anythin'?" O'Hara looked at her closely.

Sadie hesitated, then she said, "Yes, there was a man who came out of the apartment. He had some papers and a gun in his hand."

O'Hara felt the sweat break out under his arms. "Yeah?" he said. "You're sure of that?"

"Of course I'm sure."

"Would you know him again?"

"I'd know him anywhere," Sadie said firmly. "He was middle height, dark, dressed in a shabby black suit. His face was very thin, with thin lips and horrible cold eyes. I don't think I'll ever forget him."

O'Hara hadn't much time. He knew that Lu must hear about this. Grantham hadn't picked him for nothing. He had his head screwed on all right.

"Well, lady," he said, "there's been a little accident over there. I guess we'll be looking for that guy. Now will you get dressed? I'd like to take you down to the station house."

"What, now?" Sadie's eyes opened.

O'Hara nodded. "Sure," he said. "We'll get you to look through some of the photos we got down there. You might spot the guy right away."

Sadie wished Benny was there. She felt suddenly extremely helpless and alone. She didn't want to go, but she supposed she had to. "Will you wait here? I'll go and dress."

O'Hara touched his cap. "I'll meet you downstairs, lady," he said. "I don't want you bothered with newshawks. If they saw me leave with you we'd never shake them."

He went away, walking very rapidly.

Sadie dressed. She felt vaguely uneasy and wished now that she hadn't told O'Hara anything. Well, they couldn't do anything to her at the station house. She'd just tell them the truth and then they'd let her go. As she was about to leave the apartment she suddenly thought of something. She ran back to the sitting-room and scribbled a note to Benny. She put it on his pillow, hoping that if he came in he'd find it at once. Then she picked up her bag and went down to the hall.

In the meantime O'Hara met Lu, who was waiting in the street. "Listen, boss," the cop said quickly, "we're in a jam. Both Mendetta and the jane are dead, but there's a little dame up there who saw Raven leave. She can identify him. I thought you wouldn't like that. She's on her way down now. I told her I was taking her to the station."

Lu cursed under his breath. He stood thinking for a moment, then nodded. "Listen, tell her I'm a cop when she comes down. I'll take her to Grantham's apartment and he must decide what to do with her. When I've got her out of the way, continue your beat. You don't know anythin' about the killing, get it? The longer it remains under cover the better. It'll give Raven a chance to get set."

O'Hara nodded. "This'll cost me my job if it comes out," he

said with a sly look.

"Don't worry your head about that," Lu said impatiently. "We'll look after you. I'll see you get somethin' extra for this."

"See that it's worth havin'," O'Hara said, and went back into the hall.

Sadie came down as he entered. He touched his cap respectfully. "An officer of the Homicide Squad is outside with a car, lady," he said. "You go with him. I gotta do some phoning."

He led her out to Lu, who was standing by his car. Lu raised his hat.

"This is Mrs. Perminger," O'Hara said with a broad grin. "She's the little lady who saw the guy I told you about."

Lu opened the car door. "I'm sorry to get you up at such an hour, Mrs. Perminger," he said, "but you're goin' to be a big help to us."

Sadie thought he wasn't at all her idea of a plain-clothes cop, but she got in the car, because she was scared that they'd think she had something to hide. Lu got in beside her.

O'Hara stood watching the car drive away. He spat into the street. "I wonder what they'll do with her?" he thought. "Nice little dame," and he turned and resumed his patrol with measured steps.

13

June 6th, 2.30 a.m.

Carrie O'Shea ran the only high-class brothel in East St. Louis. There were plenty of other such joints in the town, but none of them came anywhere near Carrie's for class.

For one thing, it stood opposite the District Attorney's office. That alone gave it class. Then Carrie, who ran the house, saw to it that she got a fresh batch of girls each month. That wanted some doing, but Carrie knew variety is the spice of life and her clients never knew from one visit to the next who they were going to find there.

She organized the change by shuffling the girls round from the various other houses, ruthlessly selecting only the young fresh ones and refusing anything that the bookers thought they could hoist on to her.

It was only when Mendetta began his Slaving racket that Carrie really ceased to worry. Now, through a careful system, she was getting new girls pretty steadily. Of course, a lot of them made trouble, but that didn't worry Carrie a great deal. She knew how to handle girls who refused to fall in line.

The system worked this way. Trained thugs carefully combed the town for suitable girls. The qualifications that they considered suitable chiefly consisted of having no relations, being down on their luck, or to have committed some petty crime that the bookers could use as a form of blackmail.

There wasn't a great deal of material to fit these qualifications, and after a while the supply dried up. The bookers got a little more daring. They'd go after girls who wanted jobs as models. They persuaded them to pose in the nude, take photos secretly, and then threaten to show the photos, which had mysteriously become exceedingly obscene by clever faking, to narrow-minded parents. This succeeded for a time.

Although Carrie had ceased to worry about the supply of girls, the bookers were continually having headaches. They got well paid for new material, but they were constantly having to think up new ideas to ensnare unsuspecting girls into the racket.

Finally they got so bold that they'd kidnap girls and hand them over to Carrie to break in. This meant a lot more work for Carrie to do, but she realized their difficulties and she entered into her new task with philosophical fortitude.

Some of the girls were so popular that she kept them in the house as permanent workers. They had been well broken in, they got good money, and they showed no inclination to leave. Such were Andree, Lulu, Julie and Fan.

They were sitting in the big reception-room waiting patiently for Carrie to tell them to go to bed. The last client had gone over half an hour ago. Carrie made a habit of having a word with her girls before turning in for the night: to hear any complaints and to hand out punishment to any of them who hadn't given satisfaction.

The girls were all dressed in flimsy knickers, black silk stockings and high-heel shoes, with big showy garters to keep their stockings in place. They had all thrown wraps round their bare shoulders as soon as the front door closed behind the last client.Carrie thought it was all very well to sit around half naked when the guys were in the house, but when they had gone she liked to see her girls look decent.

Lulu reached for a cigarette, yawning. "Gee!" she said. "Am I tired? I've gotta get my hair fixed tomorrow morning and I don't know how I'll make it."

Fan, a red-headed girl with a superb figure, but a hard, almost brutish face, gave a short metallic laugh. "You don't want to bother about that," she said. "Get a guy to fix it for you. Do it on the exchange system."

Lulu frowned at her. "You've got a dirty mind," she said. "If I had a mind like yours I know what I'd do with it."

Julie, a little silver blonde, broke in: "Save it, you two. Let's have a little peace once in a while."

Lulu shrugged. "I'm not startin' anythin'," she said. "I'm just tellin' her she's got a dirty mind—so she has."

Julie went on, "I had the nicest and queerest guy tonight. Gee! The dough he had! When he got upstairs he was terribly shy—"

Fan groaned, "We'll now listen to a leaf out of Julie's life story."

Lulu said, "Go on, Ju, don't mind about her. Maybe she's got the crabs."

Julie pouted. "Well, I guess I won't tell you if you don't want to hear," she said. "Only he was such a nice guy-"

Fan sneered. "I know those nice guys," she said. "I've had one or two. What did he tell you? The one about his wife being an invalid?"

"Can't you leave her alone?" Lulu demanded fiercely. "What's the matter with you tonight?"

Andree, a tall brunette with long tapering limbs, gave a little giggle. "My Gawd! I saw that guy Julie's talkin' about. He looked as if his Ma was waitin' outside for him."

Julie nodded. "That's the one. He gave me ten bucks as soon as he got in the room"—she put her hand over her mouth and spluttered with laughter—"in an envelope. Can you tie that? He was so genteel he gave it to me in an envelope."

Even Fan smiled.

"Well, go on," Lulu said. "What was he like?"

Julie shook her head. "He didn't do anythin'. When I started to undress he nearly had a fit. What he thought he'd come up there for I can't guess. He said, all embarrassed, that he just wanted to talk to me. And would I put on a wrap as he thought it was tough for a girl like me to sit around as I was. Believe me, you could have knocked me over with a mangle."

"Yeah?" Fan said bitterly. "I guess I'd sooner sleep with a guy than listen to him talk. A guy who likes talkin' about it can go on for ever."

"Oh, he talked about all kinds of things. He was ever so interestin'," Julie said stoutly. "I liked the guy. He didn't once ask me why I lived here, or if I liked it, or any of the other crap guys always ask."

Fan got bored. "Gee! I thought you were goin' to tell us somethin' worth listenin' to," she said.

"Didn't I tell you she'd got a dirty mind?" Lulu chimed in triumphantly.

Just then the door opened and Carrie came in. Carrie was a tall, thin, muscular mulatto. Her face was cut in hard, etched lines. Glittering black eyes, like glass beads, gave her a look of cold, calculated suspicion and cruelty. Her broad flat nose disfigured what would have been an otherwise strikingly handsome face.

"Time you girls were in bed," she said sharply. "Break it up. Go on, get off to bed."

Obediently, all of them except Fan got up and murmured respectful good nights and went out of the door. Fan continued to sprawl in the chair.

Carrie eyed her with reluctant admiration. She had never been able to tame Fan entirely. She was wise enough to realize that Fan with a broken spirit would be a poor proposition, and she took more from her than any of the other girls put together.

She knew that Fan liked the racket. She knew also that Fan would never have admitted it, but Carrie had long ago come to realize that Fan was physically built for the game.

Carrie said, "You smoke too much. It ain't going to help you when you get older."

Fan looked at her. "Listen, nigger, I like smokin'. To hell with that stuff about getting old."

"You'll see. I'm tellin' you when you start slippin' I'll turn you out. Make no mistake, sister, I've got no time for worn-outs."

Fan got up and gathered her wrap around her. "I'll be gone long before that time," she said. "One of these days I'm goin' to start out on my own."

Carrie had heard all this before. She knew Fan was too lazy to hunt up her own clients. "Sure," she said—"one of these days."

Fan stubbed her cigarette out and then crossed to the big mirror on the wall. She stood looking at herself carefully.

Carrie grinned. She knew that Fan was secretly worried about getting old and useless. She didn't want her to be discouraged. "You're all right," she said; "one of my best girls."

Fan looked at her and sneered. "You bet, nigger," she said; "you an' I ain't the only two who know it."

She went out of the room, leaving the door wide open.

Carrie went into the little office that led from the reception-room and sat down behind a small desk. With a neat hand she entered some figures in a ledger, and then locked the ledger in a wall safe. She was quite contented the way the business was paying. Tonight had been a good one.

She looked disapprovingly at the clock on the wall. Time was always her enemy. She was a tireless worker and begrudged herself the hours wasted in sleep. But she looked after herself very carefully. She wasn't taking any chances of falling ill. Mendetta was the kind of guy who liked you a lot when you were bringing in the dough, but cast you off once you lost ground. She always gave herself six hours' sleep.

As she was getting up from behind the desk the telephone rang shrilly. She picked up the receiver. "Who is it?"

Grantham's voice floated over the line. "Carrie? Listen, I've got a girl I want you to look after."

Carrie's mouth twisted. "That's fine," she said. "Must you ring up at an hour like this to tell me a little thing like findin' me a girl? I've got plenty."

"Lu's bringing her round right away," Grantham went on. "This is important. She's not to talk to anyone. Do you understand? Hell's been poppin' tonight and she knows all about it."

"What's happened?"

"Tootsie's been bumped. Raven's taken over. And this dame

knows a hell of a lot more than she should do."

"Mendetta's dead?" Carrie repeated.

"Yeah. About a couple of hours ago. They haven't found his body yet. You're not to know anythin' about it. The news mightn't break for a couple of days."

"What's this about Raven?"

"He's moved in. You've got a new boss now, Carrie."

Carrie's fist tightened on the phone. "Why the hell did you let him move in? I tell you, Grantham, that guy's goin' to cause a lot of trouble."

"Never mind about him. You look after the girl."

Grantham hung up before she could reply.

Carrie put the phone down slowly. She stood looking at the opposite wall with blank eyes. So Raven had got there at last. She had watched him closely ever since Mendetta had turned him down. She knew that Raven would be a very different boss from Mendetta. Maybe he wouldn't be so mean, but he was going to be a lot more ruthless. Carrie suddenly found herself anxious for her girls. She didn't mind how she treated them herself, but it made her feel dismayed to think that Raven was going to control them all in the future.

She went back into the reception-room and sat down to wait for Lu.

14

June 6th, 9.30 a.m.

Jack Caston, under-manager for the local branch office of Preston Motors, walked into the Preston building with a light springy step.

The commissionaire saluted smartly and escorted him to the elevator.

Caston was the kind of guy who got up early in the morning and did breathing exercises in front of an open window. He was bouncing with good health and his big pink face was torture to anyone with a morning hang-over.

He walked into his office, rang the buzzer on his desk, and then hung up his hat. He walked over to the mirror and adjusted his tie and smoothed down his hair. He was very satisfied with what he saw in the mirror.

The door opened and his secretary walked in. She was a ritzy-looking dame, with corn-coloured hair, blue eyes, and a neat little figure.

Caston smiled at her and sat down at his desk. She thought he looked like a very nice good-humoured pig.

"Well, well," he said, stretching out his hand, "and very nice too!"

She kept her distance and inclined her head. She knew Caston.

"Now, Marie, don't be high hat. Come over here and let me look at you," he said, still keeping his hand out.

"You can see me just as well here, Mr. Caston," she said. "Did you want anything?"

Caston withdrew his hand and fiddled with a pencil. His pink face lost a little of its brightness. "Sit down," he said, "I want to talk to you."

Marie sat down, carefully adjusting her skirt as she did so. Caston leant a little forward and watched the operation with considerable interest. He considered any girl with a nice pair of legs should show them at every possible occasion.

"That's the beginning of a ladder you're getting there," he said. He leant forward, staring at her leg with fixed concentration.

Marie bent forward to investigate. She could see nothing wrong with the faultless silken hose.

"Look, just there, a little higher up. Too bad with socks as expensive as those."

Marie lifted her skirt a trifle and couldn't find anything. Caston got out of his chair and came round. "You're not lookin'," he said severely. "Look, here." He pulled her skirt well above her knees, and she promptly smacked his hand and hastily pulled it down.

"I might have known it," she said bitterly. "Just another of your tricks."

Caston beamed at her. "Well, maybe I was mistaken," he said, sitting on the edge of the desk and reaching for her hand. "But I might not have been, you know."

She allowed her hand to remain in his big pink fingers, and

she waited, her neat shoe tapping impatiently on the polished boards. "When you're through with all this," she said, "suppose we get to work?"

Caston shook his head. "I'll never train you," he said sadly. "You know, baby, you and me might get somewhere if only you'd co-operate."

Marie sniffed. "The one place I'd get to if I did would be a maternity hospital," she said acidly, snatching her hand away. "Shall we get to work?"

Caston sighed. You never knew with women. Some mornings Marie was quite willing for a little fun and games. He got off the desk and sat down in his chair. He looked at her closely. She certainly looked tired and irritable. Being a man of the world, he didn't pursue the matter, and began to dictate the few letters that required his attention.

It was ten o'clock by the time he was through, and he dismissed her with a kind smile. "Listen, baby, if you don't feel well take the rest of the day off. I've got to go out in a while and I don't think I'll be back. Just please yourself, will you?"

She looked at him suspiciously and then went out. Caston sat back in his chair and frowned. This was not starting the day well. Why the hell couldn't people be a bit more lively?

The door opened and Benny Perminger wandered in. Caston gave him a quick look and groaned. This was certainly not going to be his day. Benny was looking like something the cat had dug up.

"And what's your trouble?" he asked shortly.

Benny sank into the arm-chair and sighed. "Nice bit that, ain't she?" he said, pursing up his mouth.

Caston frowned. "Who's a nice bit?" he demanded.

"Miss Mackelsfield," Benny explained. "Lucky guy havin' a secretary like that."

"Well, I don't know," Caston said. "What of it?"

Benny closed one eye and leered. "You bachelors," he said; "I bet you an' she have a grand time."

Caston sat up stiffly. "Now see here, Perminger, I don't like that kind of talk. This is a business place, and business only is conducted here."

"Nuts! What kind of business? All you guys do in these offices is to horse around with your secretaries. I know. It's guys like me out in the general office that don't get the chances."

Caston thought it wise to shift the ground. "Well, you didn't come in here to tell me that, did you?"

Benny's face fell, and he became depressed again. "No," he admitted, "I didn't. As a matter of fact, Caston, old boy, I came for a little advice."

Caston smiled. Things were looking up. He liked giving advice. He settled back in his chair and lit a cigarette. "Sure," he said. "What's the trouble?" For a moment he had a sudden qualm that Benny was going to touch him for some dough, but on second thoughts he knew that wasn't Benny's usual opening when he made a touch.

Benny hung his feet over the side of the chair. "Well, Sadie and I have had a quarrel," he said bitterly. "She properly shot her mouth off last night."

Caston made sympathetic noises. "Nice girl, Sadie," he said. He often wondered why a swell looker like Sadie had fallen for Perminger. He could have gone a long way to have made her himself.

"Sure, she's a nice girl, but she's got a damn odd way of looking at things. Would you believe it, she's accusing me of always lookin' at girls? She even had the neck to say that I'd be makin' a pass at one of them one day."

Caston shrugged. "Well, won't you?"

Benny looked vacant. "Well, yes, I suppose I will," he admitted. "But she won't know about it."

"Listen, Perminger, wasn't that a dame I saw you out with the other night?"

Benny scowled at him. "What else do you think it was?" he snapped. "A horse?"

"Steady, buddy," Caston said. "No need to go off the deep end. What I meant was, she wasn't Sadie?"

Benny shook his head. "No, she was a business client. She wanted to buy one of our models."

Caston blew his nose. "I suppose you were taking a fly out of her eye?" he said sarcastically.

"Will you leave it? I want your advice, not a goddamn sermon," Benny returned. "I've walked out and left Sadie high and dry. What the hell am I going to do?"

"You've left her?" Caston asked, his eyebrows raising. "You

crazy or something?"

"I tell you we had a stand-up fight. I couldn't just go to bed after it."

"You left her all night?" Caston wished he'd known that. He might have called and done himself some good.

"What I want you to bend your brains on is how am I going back?"

Caston shrugged. "Easiest thing in the world. All you do is to walk in, kiss her, tell her you were tight and all will be well."

Benny stared at him. "Do you really think so?" he asked. "Gee! I wish it would work like that."

Caston was getting a little bored, anyway. "Sure," he said, getting up, "you try it. Don't forget, she might be pretty sick about it herself today. You go down there right away. You might find her in."

Benny got to his feet. "I'll do it. That's mighty white of you, Jack. If there's any little thing—"

Caston led him to the door. "On your way, pal," he said, "and if it works, give her one for me."

He watched Benny hurry down the corridor before turning back to his office.

15

June 6th, 9.45 a.m.

Raven sat on the edge of his bed and looked round at the three men who stood or leant against the wall opposite him.

There was Lefty, Little Joe and Maltz. For eighteen months these three men had elected to follow Raven, and they had for this period experienced a very thin time. Raven didn't excuse himself. He had just told them to be patient and they had believed him. He had never let them go hungry. Somehow, by dangerous raids, hold-ups and the like, they had managed to make a little money, but all the same they had all had a bad time. Such was their faith in Raven, however, that they had not grumbled. It was now that he could tell them that their faith in him was justified.

He knew these three men for what they were. There was no

spark of human feeling in any of them. They wanted money: not just money, but big money. They didn't care how they got it, but they knew that none of them had the brains to make that money. They knew Raven could make it, so they had been contented to wait.

Raven looked round at them, and he gloried in his triumph. "Well," he said, "I've sent for you guys because somethin's happenin'. I told you it would, and it has."

The three shifted a little and regarded him with blank, stony eyes. Three jaws moved rhythmically as they turned the chewing-gum in their mouths.

"When I first came to this burg I wanted to play ball with Mendetta. But the dirty rat said no. He was in the position to say no. I had to take it. You guys thought I'd get a break. You've stuck around for a long time waiting for that break. You haven't bellyached. You've done what I've told you—well, by God, we've waited long enough. We're takin' over the burg."

Still the three stood silent. They waited for facts.

"Mendetta had protection," Raven said, stressing the past tense. "We couldn't start anythin' as long as he was alive. Now he's dead—so we move in."

The three fidgeted.

"I've seen Grantham. He won't be any trouble. In a day or so I'll have my hands on some dough. We're goin' to organize this burg. We're goin' to milk it dry. We've got everythin' just where we want it. I'm tellin' you what to do, an' you'll do it. That way we'll all be in the dough."

Maltz, a little wop, with a heavy sneering mouth and bloodshot black eyes, straightened away from the—wall. "You said you'd do it, boss," he said, "and we knew you would. Why didn't you get one of us to rub Mendetta?"

Raven shook his head. "Who said I killed him?" he asked quietly.

The three exchanged glances and grinned. They thought that was a good joke.

Raven got to his feet. "Stick around, fellas," he said, "I gotta go an' talk with Grantham. By tonight I'll know how much dough's comin' to us."

He went away, leaving them still standing in his bedroom.

16

June 6th, 10.30 a.m.

Johnson, the desk sergeant, chewed the end of his pen and regarded Jay with an unfavourable eye. He never had much use for crime reporters. They were always bobbing up at the wrong time and always asking embarrassing questions. Jay was no exception to this. In fact, he showed a lot of talent for being a nuisance.

Jay, with his hands full of petty and uninteresting crimes, was feeling irritable. He wanted a free hand to work on the Mendetta affair. The fact that Poison had warned him to lay off did not deter him. He was as determined to go ahead and find out what had happened to Fletcher's sister as he had been before hearing Poison's threat of dismissal. He knew he was good as a reporter and he knew he wouldn't have far to look for another job. What did rile him was the number of small cases that had suddenly arisen during the night which he was bound to cover, and now he found himself chained by the leg to the station house, awaiting fresh evidence. It looked like he'd be there all the morning. Then he had to write up his two columns, so Fletcher's sister would have to wait until the evening.

Johnson sighed. "It's a pity your paper can't find you a job of work to do," he said sourly. "I'm gettin' tired of seein' you loafin' around this joint. Why don't you go out an' take a little exercise?"

Jay put his feet up on the wooden bench and closed his eyes. "Leave me alone," he said. "I'm sick of breathin' the same air as you, but this is what I'm bein' paid for, so leave out the cracks."

The sergeant grunted and began to write laboriously in the charge book. "Well, there ain't much about," he said, blotting his neat writing carefully. "You guys live pretty soft, I must say."

"It's when there's nothin' about that we work hard," Jay told him. "Look what we've got today. Petty thieving, an embezzlement, and a small-time forger. How would you like to make a column out of that little lot? What I want is a nice rape or a good murder. Somethin' that'll take my column on the front page."

Johnson scowled. "Horrible lot you newspaper guys," he said.

"Do you know how many girls have been reported missing this year?" Jay asked.

Johnson shook his head. "Not my department," he said promptly. "You want the Missing People's Bureau. You lost someone?"

Jay shook his head. "I was wonderin', Johnson, if there's anythin' in this White Slave rumour I've heard about."

Johnson laughed. "Not a word," he said. "You think about it for a moment and you'll see that there can't be anythin' in it."

"You tell me. It'll save my energies."

Johnson spread himself over his desk and folded his arms on his blotter. "It's like these rape cases we get," he explained. "It ain't possible to rape a woman against her will. In the same way, it ain't possible to keep a woman in prostitution against her will in a big city like this. Sooner or later we should hear complaints. Guys that go to these houses would report that a woman was being held against her will. But we never hear of them. Obviously, the women are in the game for what they get out of it, and the stories we hear about Slaving is so much junk."

Jay considered this. "Suppose these women were terrorized?" he said. "How about that?"

Johnson shook his head. "Too risky," he said. "We'd give them protection if they wanted to squawk. All they have to do is to walk in here, lodge a complaint, and we'd look after them until an investigation's been made."

"Suppose they can't get out?" Jay persisted.

Johnson frowned. "What you hintin' at?" he demanded. "Do you know anythin'?"

Jay shook his head. "Nope," he confessed; "but I'm interested. I believe that a woman could be terrorized into prostitution, and I'm lookin' into it from this angle. I may be wrong, but if I ain't, I'm going to keep you mighty busy bookin' the heels who run the racket."

"You're wasting your time," Johnson said. "What you want is an excuse to play around with undesirable floosies. I bet part of your investigation will be meetin' and talkin' to these dames."

Jay shook his head. "I'm serious, Johnson," he said. "You wait and see. If I do strike on anythin' you'd better get ready for some heavy work."

A police officer came in, followed by Benny Perminger. The officer went up to Johnson. "This guy thinks we've got his wife in gaol," he said. "Will you speak to him?"

Johnson looked at Benny doubtfully. "What's the trouble?" he demanded.

Benny was looking scared. "I'm Ben Perminger," he said. "I want to see my wife."

Johnson closed his mouth into a thin line. "I ain't stoppin' you," he said coldly. "She ain't here."

"Well, where have you taken her?"

"What is all this?"

Benny began to look bewildered. "Well, I don't know," he said. "I found this note when I got home." He gave Johnson a slip of paper.

Jay sat up on the bench and watched all this with interest. He smelt a news story.

Johnson read the note and handed it back. "There's no one of the name of Perminger booked last night. We didn't pull anyone in from that address. I guess she's havin' a game with you."

Benny stood staring at the note. "Maybe they didn't bring her here. Could they take her anywhere else?"

"There's the station on West 47th Street. I'll ask them." Johnson pulled the phone towards him and put the enquiry through. After a short wait he shook his head and hung up. "No, they don't know anythin' about it."

Benny began to sweat. "What am I goin' to do?" he asked.

Johnson was getting bored with him. "It's your wife, buddy," he said. "Most like she's havin' a little game with you. You go back home. You'll find her waitin' for you."

Benny turned away from the desk and moved slowly towards the door.

Johnson looked at Jay. "That guy's got a leak in his conk," he said under his breath.

Jay got up and followed Benny out of the station house, ignoring Johnson's yell for him to come back.

Benny walked down the street in a daze. He didn't know

what to make of it. Surely Sadie wouldn't pull a stunt like this if it didn't mean anything? She had said that she was being taken down to the station house as a witness and would Benny come at once.

Jay overtook him at the comer. "Hey, Perminger," he said, "what's all this about your wife?"

Benny blinked at him. "Where the hell did you spring from?" he said, shaking hands.

"Come over an' have a drink," Jay said, taking him by his arm and steering him into a near-by bar. "I overheard what you were tellin' Johnson. What's happened to Mrs. P.?"

Seated at a small table away from the bar and assisted by a large iced beer, Benny unburdened. He told Jay how he had quarrelled with Sadie and how he'd left her during the night. "Well, I felt a bit of a heel this morning," he went on, "so I thought I'd get back and make it up. When I got in I found all the lights burning and a note on my pillow saying she'd been taken down to headquarters as a witness and would I please come." He paused to pull at his beer.

Jay puzzled. On the face of it, he thought, Sadie might be just teaching this guy a lesson, but his instinct for news was not satisfied. Why should she use such an odd way of scaring him? Why a witness? A witness of what? No, it didn't quite add up.

"I thought the police were supposed to help you," Benny grumbled. "The way that guy went on, you'd think I was crazy."

"You don't have to worry about him. He's gettin' all kinds of stories and complaints every hour, and he just doesn't take any interest. Where are you livin' now?"

Benny told him.

Jay suddenly sat up. "Surely, that's where Tootsie Mendetta hangs out?" he said.

Benny nodded. "That's right," he answered. "I've been wantin' an introduction to him for weeks. I want to sell him a flock of tracks. He lives just opposite my apartment, but I've never set eyes on him."

Jay got to his feet. There might be something in this story after all. It was a long shot, but he wasn't going to let it grow cold. "We'll go back to your apartment and have a look round," he said. "Come on, buddy, let's go."

Benny went with him and they took a taxi to the block.

Inside his apartment Jay couldn't find anything that excited him. It was just an ordinary joint of a man with a nice income. He wandered around, his hands deep in his trouser pockets, brooding.

Benny sat on the arm of a chair and watched him.

"Did she take a suit-case or anythin'?" Jay asked suddenly.

Benny looked bewildered. "I don't know," he said. "I hadn't thought of lookin'."

"Check that up, will you, pal?"

Benny went into the bedroom and after a while he came out again. He looked more bewildered still. He shook his head helplessly. "No," he said, "she hasn't taken anythin'. The only things that are missing are the clothes she wore yesterday and her handbag. Nothing else."

Jay didn't like the sound of this. No woman would ran away from her husband without taking some of her belongings.

"Will you wait here?" he said. "I'll go across and hare a word with Mendetta. Maybe he heard somethin'."

Benny suddenly went very pale. "You don't think anythin' bad's happened to her?" he asked.

Jay shook his head. "No," he said, "I don't think so, but we'll clear this up or find out somethin', so we can get the cops interested. You sit down for a moment."

He left the apartment and crossed the corridor. He rang Mendetta's bell. No one answered. He stood there waiting, and then he rang again. Still no one answered.

Benny came to his front door and stood watching him.

"No one seems at home," he said.

Jay scratched his head. "Will you phone down to the porter and find out what time Mendetta went out?" he said.

While Benny was doing this Jay took a little instrument from his vest pocket and inserted it in the lock. He made no attempt to open the door, but by careful probing he knew that, if he wanted to, he could do so.

Benny came back, looking blank. "The porter guy says Mendetta hasn't left the building."

Jay put his thumb on the bell and kept it there. They stood listening to the angry whirr of the bell for several minutes. Then Jay made up his mind. "I'm goin' in," he said.

"You can't do that. Maybe he's asleep."

Jay looked at him. "I'm chancin' that," he said shortly. "Somehow, I feel there's somethin' wrong in there."

He once more probed with his instrument and a moment later the lock slid back with a little snick. Gently, he eased the door back and looked into the hall. Then he stepped in softly and entered the first room he came to.

He stood looking at Mendetta sprawled out on the floor. His big head rested in a pool of blood. Over the other side of the room Jean lay, one leg drawn up and her arms flung wide. Jean wasn't very nice to look at.

Jay caught his breath. Here was his front page murder. He spun on his heel and nearly collided with Benny, who had come in.

"My God!" Benny said, going suddenly very green.

Jay pushed him out into the corridor. "Keep your shirt on," he said roughly. "Go into your apartment and get some drinks lined up."

Benny went away hurriedly, and Jay carefully closed the apartment door. He followed Benny and grabbed the telephone. "Listen," he said, as he hastily dialled a number, "there's goin' to be a riot in a little while. Did your wife know Mendetta?"

Benny gave himself a long drink of Scotch. He shook his head. "You don't think she's mixed up in this, do you?"

Jay was already on to Henry. "Mendetta's been bumped," he said. "I've just been into his apartment. We've got the exclusive story. Even the cops don't know yet. Can you get this story on the street right away?"

Henry got very excited. "Let's have it," he said.

Jay sat down. In short, crisp sentences he fired off the discovery of finding Mendetta's and Jean's bodies.

"What the hell were you doin' up there?" Henry snapped.

"I'll fix that end," Jay told him. "You get that on the street in ten minutes and you'll beat the whole gang to it. I've got to tell the cops."

"When you're through come on back. I've got to see what Poison's got to say about this."

"To hell with Poison. This is the story of my life. If Poison's going to put a soft pedal on it I'm quittin'," and Jay hung up.

He turned to Benny. "Listen, pal, this is where you've got to be a big help. We're goin' down to get the porter to open

Mendetta's door. It wouldn't look too good if they found out that I've broken in. Come on, we've gotta work fast."

Protesting feebly, Benny followed him downstairs.

17

June 6th, 11 a.m.

Sadie opened her eyes. The hard, naked light of the electric lamp blinded her and she rolled over on the bed, shielding her eyes with her arm. A stabbing pain shot through her head as she moved.

She couldn't think where she was or what had happened to her. Her mouth felt dry and her body ached. She lay for some time, only half conscious. Then, after a while, her mind began to function again. She remembered dimly leaving her home. She remembered Lu. Out of the mists Grantham's face appeared—Grantham, thin-lipped, standing over her with something in his hand that she couldn't see. She remembered her terror, and, as she started to scream, a hot hand coming from behind her, over her mouth. She remembered a sharp prick in her arm and her wild struggle, then she remembered nothing more.

Again she half opened her eyes. She was aware that she was lying on a mattress and the colour of the walls was a drab grey. Her heart began to thud wildly. It was no horrible nightmare, then. She turned over and looked round the room.

It was small. The thick carpet on the floor matched the walls. There was no other furniture in the room except the bed on which she was lying.

The door was opposite her. Slowly she sat up, holding her head between her hands. There was something the matter with the room. For a moment she couldn't make it out, then she realized that there was no window. The discovery did a lot to clear her brain. She knew that she was in acute danger. Of what she didn't know, but all the same it made her sick with terror.

Slowly she got off the bed and staggered across the room to the door. Her feet sank into the pile of the carpet, which deadened her footfalls. She tried the door, but it was locked. She stood pulling weakly at the handle, and then she slid down on to the floor and began to cry.

Her head hurt so. She was so frightened. Where could she be? she asked herself. She stayed like that for some time, and when she couldn't cry any more she again got control of her nerves. She knew she would get nowhere just crying, and, taking herself in hand, she stood up.

She tried the door, pulling at the handle without success, and then she hammered on the panels. That gave her a horrible shock. The panels were covered with a thick layer of rubber. Her small fists bounced back every time she struck, and she could make no sound as she hammered.

She turned and stumbled blindly to the opposite wall and put her hands on it. Rubber again. The room was sound-proof, lined with heavy rubber, even to the ceiling.

She knew then that something horribly was going to happen to her, and she began to scream wildly.

18

June 6th, 12 noon.

Raven came out of the 22nd Club and signalled to a taxi. His thin white face was expressionless, but there was a triumphant gleam in his eyes. He carried a leather document case, and he climbed into the taxi with a new dignity that off-set his shabby clothes. He gave the address of his hotel and sat back.

The taxi was a symbol of his success. He hadn't ridden in a taxi since he'd left Chi. Now things were going to be different. In the document case were papers that made him a rich man. Grantham hadn't raised any objection. He had turned Mendetta's shares over to him without a word. They were all bearer bonds. Nothing to connect Raven with him. But they meant money. He had been willing to have shared all this with Mendetta, but the rat had said no. Now he had it all.

The taxi swerved and pulled up outside the hotel. Raven paid him off and hurried upstairs. The three were waiting for him, still chewing, blank, stolid expressions on their faces.

Raven looked round at them and they in turn looked at him. He raised the case so that they could see it. He knew it was no use explaining anything about holdings or shares or bearer bonds to them. They hadn't the mentality to understand. All they could understand was money. Not in cheques or bonds, but in notes and coin.

He took from his pocket his small, fast-vanishing roll. He peeled off two notes and gave them to Little Joe. "Go and get some Scotch," he said. "Get glasses from downstairs. Make it snappy."

A little grin came to the faces of the three. This they could understand. A guy doesn't buy them one drink, he sends for a bottle. That must mean dough.

While Little Joe was away Raven took off his hat and combed his hair carefully. He adjusted his frayed tie and regarded himself for a long while in the fly-blown mirror.

The other two watched him with interest. Raven took no notice of them; he was waiting for Little Joe. They knew this and were content to wait. Little Joe had tagged along with them; he was entitled to hear what was to be said as much as the others.

Little Joe came back with the Scotch and glasses. At a sign from Raven he poured drinks out all round.

Raven took his glass. "Money and power," he said, and they all drank.

Sitting down, Raven ht a cigarette. "It's fixed," he said. "We're movin' to the St. Louis Hotel right away. When we're settled we can look around for somethin' better, but that'll do to get along with."

The St. Louis Hotel was the best hotel in town.

Maltz said, "Gee! That joint's too swell for us guys."

"You've got to change your ideas—all of you. This is no longer a small-town party. We're big shots," Raven said, sipping his whisky carefully. "I want to talk to you guys. We're startin' work right away. You've got to go round the bars and spread the rumour that all whores are to get off the streets or else... Do you get it?"

Little Joe scratched his head. "Say, what's the idea?"

Raven knew he'd got to be patient with these guys. "We're goin' to clean up the whole town. It's goin' to be a hell of a job, but it's got to be done. You three have got to get so many hoods in each district of the town who are tough enough to run the whores off the streets and to deal with their bookers. That's your first job. I'll make myself plain. What happens to a guy who smokes a lot and suddenly finds out he can't get tobacco?"

Lefty knew that one. "He goes nuts," he said simply.

Raven nodded. "That's it, he goes nuts. Then supposing some guy comes along and offers him tobacco after a while at a greatly increased price? What happens?"

The three looked at each other. This was getting beyond them.

"He pays more because he can't get it elsewhere," Raven said patiently.

"So what?" Little Joe said.

"That's what we're goin' to do. Once we get organized, no whore on the streets will be safe. She's got to be treated rough, so she's too scared to work. We want them to leave town. It'll take a little while, but if you treat 'em rough enough they'll go. If they don't, then we've got to start shootin', but that'll be the last straw. We don't want trouble with the cops. If we knock 'em about, cut 'em a little, the cops won't do anythin', but if we kill 'em, then they'll have to get busy."

"It's goin' to be tough on the guys who like whores," Maltz said, thinking of himself.

"Now you're gettin' somewhere," Raven said. "We're goin' to set up houses. Not these fancy brothels that Mendetta ran. There's no big dough in those. He took a ten per cent cut on the house. The girls got fifty and the rest of the dough was put into expenses. That's a crazy way of workin' it. I'm doin' it differently." He edged forward. "Each girl will be paid a fixed salary. She'll never see the dough. It'll be put to her credit in a ledger. Out of this she'll have to pay rent for her room, her clothes, smokes, drinks and whatever else she wants. The balance, if there is a balance, will be used to buy shares in the house to give her a business interest." Raven smiled crookedly. "When she wants to go she can sell out at the market price—which will be fixed by me—and she can beat it."

Lefty understood a little of this. "She doesn't see any dough at all, then?"

"That's right. I'm using that dough as capital."

"These dames like to see money. They won't like this, boss."

Raven smiled. His thin lips just showed his teeth. It was more of a grimace than a smile. "They're not supposed to like it," he said. "They're goin' to do as they're told."

The three exchanged glances. "Rough stuff again, boss?" Little Joe asked.

"Ever been to Reno?" Raven said. "I have. Know what they do to a dame who won't play ball? They pour turpentine on her belly. They play ball all right after that."

There was a long silence. The three digested that piece of information. "I guess that hurts all right," Lefty said. "Gee! I'd hate that to happen to me."

"It wouldn't hurt you as it hurts them," Raven said.

"You think about it." He got to his feet. "I'm goin' to the bank to get some dough. I'll stake you guys to a roll. You've got to get yourselves some new clothes. Don't forget you're livin' at the St. Louis from now on. When you're fixed you've got to start work." He broke off abruptly and stood listening.

The others sat very still.

Through the closed window they could hear a lot of shouting in the street. Raven took two quick steps to the window and threw it up. He looked down and then turned away.

"It's out," he said briefly. His eyes were very bright. "They're tellin' the world that Mendetta's dead."

The others made a move to the window, but he stopped them. "You've got to work fast now," he said. "The sooner we're organized the quicker we make dough."

He went out of the room hurriedly.

The three made a dash to the window. Across the road they could see a newsvendor standing busily handing out papers. When the crowd thinned a little they could read his placard:

MENDETTA AND MOLL SHOT TO DEATH

Lefty heaved a big sigh. "Didn't I tell you that guy was somethin'?" he said proudly.

19

June 6th, 12.5 p.m.

Grantham's office door burst open and Lu came in. He shut the door hurriedly and waved a newspaper. "It's out already," he said excitedly. "Look, boss, they're playin' it on the front page."

Grantham reached out and took the paper. He glanced at it and then tossed it on one side. "Quicker than I thought," he said, lighting a cigarette. "There's goin' to be a lot of guys yellin' at me very soon."

Lu sat on the edge of the desk. "That dame Perminger," he said. "Was it the right thing to turn her over to Carrie?"

Grantham looked at him coldly. "Why not?"

"Suppose she gets away an' talks?"

"What do you want me to do? Finish her?"

Lu nodded. "That would have been a lot safer."

"Listen, I'm the guy with brains. I want to keep that dame just where I can reach her in a hurry. You and I are under Raven now. As long as he brings in the dough, it's all right with us. Have you thought that, maybe, he won't succeed? Suppose we don't get anythin' better out of this change-over? Would you like the job of shifting Raven?"

Lu glanced away. "Where's this leadin' to?"

"As long as we've got a witness that Raven killed Mendetta we've got Raven where we want him. If he slips, then the Perminger dame goes to the cops with my love."

"Yeah? And she spills that you've been holding her in a knockin'-shop."

Grantham's thin mouth twisted into a smile. "She'll do what she's told, and she'll say what I want her to say."

Lu raised his eyebrows. "She may be tough," he said.

"Carrie likes 'em tough." Grantham reached forward and knocked the ash off his cigarette. "I've told her to start softenin' her as soon as she comes to the surface. Carrie knows her job."

"If Raven gets to hear about this it's goin' to be just too bad for you."

"Raven won't hear about it. Carrie knows me well enough not to open her mouth. You're the only other one. If you say anythin' to him you'll only do yourself dirt. You an' me get along all right, don't we?"

Lu nodded. "Sure," he said. "I was just thinkin' of Carrie."

The phone bell rang sharply. Grantham picked it up.

A girl said, "Judge Hennessey wants you."

"Put him on the line," Grantham said. "It's that old heel Hennessey," he whispered to Lu.

Hennessey's voice sounded agitated. "What's this about Mendetta?" he demanded. "Is it true?"

"Yes, Judge, I guess it's true all right. He was shot last night."

"Who did it?"

"We ah want to know that." Grantham winked at Lu.

"Listen, Grantham, what are you doin' about it? I want to know where I stand. Who's goin' to take over?"

"It's all right, Judge, Tootsie fixed everything up with me months ago. He was expectin' trouble. Yeah, he left everythin' in my hands."

"In your hands?" Hennessey's voice sounded doubtful. "Can you carry on?"

"Sure I can carry on. Mendetta left everythin' straightforward. The thing runs itself now, Judge."

"I see." There was a long pause, then he went on, "You been through the books yet?"

"Just this minute startin' on them, Judge. You don't have to worry. We want guys like you around."

"Of course you do," the Judge snapped. "Your outfit would look mighty sick without me. Mendetta sent it to me on the first of the month. You'd better do the same."

"That's okay with me, Judge. First of the month? Sure, it'll be along."

"Well, I wish you luck, Grantham. Maybe it does run on its own power. You watch it, won't you?"

"I'll watch it." Grantham hung up. "Rat number one," he said, pursing his mouth. "Wanted to know if his rake-off was to continue. Didn't care a damn that Tootsie was dead. Just dough."

Lu grinned. "It ain't every organization who's got a Judge in its pocket," he said. "That guy may be expensive, but he's done some nice work for us."

Grantham unlocked a drawer in his desk and took out a little leather-bound note-book. He flicked through the pages and then, finding what he was looking for, he studied the page carefully. "Yeah," he said; "last year he had seventeen of our girls before him. Twelve dismissals, four warnings and one small fine. Yeah, I guess he's worth the dough all right."

Once more the phone rang. "Yeah?" Grantham said, again picking up the receiver. "Yeah, it's Grantham speaking. Is that you, Mr. Hackensfield?... How are you?... Mendetta? Sure we know he's dead.... Yeah, too bad.... No, you don't have to worry.... Sure we want you to work along with us. First of the month?... Yeah, we're lookin' into it right now.... Sure you're useful.... That's all right, Mr. Hackensfield. It'll be along." He hung up.

Lu said, "They like their dough, these guys." Grantham nodded. "The District Attorney wanted to know if Mendetta's death was goin' to make any difference to his income," he said, leaning back in his chair. "This is goin' on all day, Lu. I may as well get used to it."

"Are you makin' any changes?"

Grantham shook his head. "Raven's seen the list. He wants it to go on for a time. When that guy's settled down he might start somethin'. He's wise. He's waitin' until he's strong enough to get tough."

Lu moved towards the door as the phone went again. "I'll leave you to it, boss," he said. "See you in church." He went out of the office.

Grantham grimaced and picked up the phone. "Mr. Poison wants you, Mr. Grantham," a girl said.

"Put him through." A cold, hard gleam came into Grantham's voice. "Grantham?"

"That's right. I wanted a little word with you, Mr. Poison.... Sure—about Mendetta. You're wonderin' about those shares?... So am I.... That's right, I said I was wonderin' too.... Sure I've taken over. Mendetta left everythin' in my hands.... Why? Well, I'm the only guy who knows how the business is run.... That's right."

Poison said furiously, "He's crazy to have left it to you. You don't understand this business, Grantham. I've got to safeguard my investment. You've got to find someone who can look after the outside organization. You stick around all day in the Club. You've got to have someone outside watching those women. They're lazy by nature. Mendetta understood them. He got the best out of them."

Grantham smiled unpleasantly. "Take it easy," he said. "I told you I'm runnin' this business, and I am. I don't care a damn about anythin' you say, so leave off throwin' your weight around."

"By God! You can't talk to me like this," Poison exploded. "Half my money's financing this business, and I've got a right to say how it should be run."

"You've got a right to receive dividends when they come due," Grantham said sharply, "but that's all. I'm the boss around here and don't you forget it."

"You be careful how you talk to me," Poison said, his voice thick with rage. "A word in the right direction would make things mighty unpleasant for you."

Grantham laughed. "Forget it, Poison," he jeered. "You can't scare me with that stuff. What about you? How would you look if it got around that half your money comes from brothel investments? I've got your signatures, don't forget."

There was a long pause, then Poison said more mildly: "Don't let us quarrel, Grantham."

Grantham nodded. "We won't quarrel. Don't you worry about the business. If it doesn't keep up its returns I promise you I'll have a talk with you in three months' time—how's that?"

"Very well. I'll see how you manage for three months."

"By the way, Poison, how come your paper was the first on the street with the news?"

"I'm not responsible for that," Poison said, his voice sinking to a very mild note. "I've got a crime reporter who's pretty good on his job."

"Yeah? He's too good, Poison. He's cut my working time down badly. I reckoned on another twenty-four hours to get organized. There might be a little trouble with the bookers now."

"He knows all about it," Poison said grimly. "I've told him to lay off the case."

"It's a bit late now," Grantham said. "I suppose it's Jay Ellinger?"

"Yes, do you know him?"

"I know him all right. He's been snoopin' around a little too much lately. Can't you send him out of town?"

"Well, I could."

"I'd like you to do that. He makes me nervous. Can't you send him somewhere out of the way for a little while? I want time to get organized, and I think he's gettin' a little too near the truth."

Poison thought a moment. "Yeah," he said, "I'll get him to cover the Tammany Hall trial. That'll keep him in New York for at least a month. Every paper is sending a reporter. He can't refuse to go. I could get him on the black list if he did."

Grantham sighed with relief. "Do that, Poison, and I'll guarantee you results."

"Consider it done," Poison said, and hung up.

Grantham replaced the receiver and relaxed. So far as he could see it was going all right. It depended a lot on Raven. If Raven's ideas were good the organization would hold together. After all, Mendetta had built it up on sound lines. He had over two hundred girls working for him. He had the Club, which paid very well, and his protection rackets were bringing in big dough. Yes, on the face of it it looked all right.

Grantham reached for another cigarette as the phone rang again.

20

June 6th, 2.45 p.m.

Benny made up his mind to get drunk. He couldn't take any more. From the time Jay called the Homicide Bureau he had been pushed around as if he'd been the one who had shot Mendetta.

Cold-eyed cops had come into his apartment and looked him over. They had asked him questions about Sadie. They wanted to know where she was. When he showed them the letter she'd written they didn't believe a word of it.

Carter, the officer-in-charge, had taken him into a corner. "See here, Perminger, your tale stinks. Why was Mrs. Perminger alone in this apartment all night?"

Benny clutched his head. "I keep tellin' you," he groaned, "she an' I had a tiff. So I walked out on her."

"What was the quarrel about?"

Benny tried to explain, but Carter sneered at him. "You mean to tell me that you walked out of this joint because your wife objected to you lookin' at dames? Now, think about it. Isn't that the lousiest story you've ever heard?"

"Well, it wasn't only that. She an' I were at the fights, an' by accident I got my head between some dame's knees—"

Carter's eyes bulged. "You did what?" he said.

Benny wrenched at his collar. "Yeah, that's right. You see, she was sittin' right behind me..."

Carter turned away. "Hi, Murphy, this guy's got a hot one here. He goes around sticking his head between dames' knees."

Murphy raised his eyebrows. "Well, tell him to stop doin' it. Tell him one thing leads to another."

Carter scowled at Benny. "You gotta be careful what you do, guy," he said. "We can't take you in for that, but mind it's your head next time."

And so it went on. The cops were far too excited looking at the dead bodies of Jean and Mendetta, hunting through the desk and drawers, to be really interested in Benny. When he tried to bring up about Sadie they told him to go down to the Missing People's Bureau.

Finally he gave up and sat down to wait for them to go. When they were through photographing the bodies, testing for finger-prints and ransacking the apartment. Carter found a little time to speak to him again.

He said, "We'll want you, buddy, so stick around. There's goin' to be a big stink over this, an' you're goin' to be right in the middle of it. When we want you we'll send for you."

They all went off after that and left Benny alone. So he decided to get good and drunk.

A little while later Jay found him, sitting in his armchair, a bottle of Scotch by his side and a glass clutched firmly in his hand.

Jay looked at him. "Hey, soak," he said, "anythin' left for me?"

Benny got hastily to his feet. "Am I glad to see you?" he said, shaking hands vigorously. "Sure, have a drink. I'll get you a glass."

Jay pushed him back into the chair. "I'll get it," he said. "You take it easy."

When he came back from the kitchen, holding a glass, Benny had just given himself a long shot.

"Wait a minute," Jay said hastily, taking the bottle away. "You've got to keep sober for a while." He poured himself out two fingers and sat down on the edge of the table. "Listen, buddy, I want to talk to you."

Benny shook his head. "I can't stand any more of it," he said. "Those cops have been making my conk buzz."

"Never mind about the cops. You an' me've got a job of work to do. You want to find your wife, don't you?"

"Why, goddamn it, of course I do."

"All right, then. Now listen. You don't know anythin' about how a murder is investigated. Well, I do. I've been watchin' these guys. They're puttin' on a front. They don't want to find out who killed Mendetta. They don't want to find out where your wife is. So they fool around, ask a lot of bull questions and then leave it at that. Maybe they'll forget all about you."

Benny sobered. "That's cock-eyed," he said. "It's their job to find out things like that."

Jay smiled grimly. "That's what you think, but you don't know anythin'. This is serious, Perminger. If you're not ready to do somethin' your wife'll never be found."

"What have I got to do?"

"I'll explain things so you can understand. Do you know what Mendetta did for a livin'?"

Benny shook his head. "I know he'd got plenty of dough," he said. "And I've heard he was mixed up with some rackets. What they are I don't know."

Jay nodded. "Well, I'll tell you. He was runnin' brothels."

Benny blinked. "You sure of that?" he said.

"I'm sure."

"Mind you, I wouldn't like to earn my dough that way, but brothels are necessary, ain't they?"

"Not Mendetta's brothels. I've heard he fills them by Slave methods. I don't want to scare you, buddy, but I think your wife's in one of his houses right now."

Benny stared at him. "What!" he said.

Jay nodded. "I think so, Perminger."

"You're crazy!" Benny said, his voice rising. He got to his feet. "That's a goddamn dirty lie, and you know it. Take it back, you heel, or I'll kick the nuts off you."

Jay reached out and shoved him in his chest. Benny flopped over into the chair again. "Quiet," Jay said. "You've got to listen to this. You don't know how deep it goes."

Benny said between his teeth, "You're goin' to be sorry for this, you heel!"

"Aw, shut up; let me tell you. Mendetta's dead. Who killed him? Some guy who thinks he can make more dough out of the racket. There's Grantham at 22nd Club. It might be he, but I don't think so. He hasn't the guts. Never mind who it is just yet. Mendetta's girls never had a conviction. Time after time I've been in court when one of them was brought in for soliciting, and every time they got off. Every time one of his girls came up Judge Hennessey was the guy who found them not guilty. Why? Ever heard of corrupt judges? All right. Mendetta must have had a lot of protection. That means he paid out a lot of dough. When he was killed, I'm bettin' those guys who got regular dough started gettin' scared. If they find the guy who killed Mendetta they won't get any more easy dough. They're givin' him a run. If he keeps up payment, as Mendetta did, then he's safe. That's the way the racket is worked in this town."

Benny said, "What the hell has it to do with Sadie?"

Jay leant forward. "Suppose Sadie saw the killer? Suppose she reported it to the cops? Suppose they got excited and saw that she was goin' to bust up their racket? What would they do? Give her a cake and a bronx cheer? Like hell!"

Benny sat very still. "What could they do with her?"

"They could either knock her on the head or else give her over to Grantham. You've got to face it, Perminger. If her body ain't found in a week or so, then she's in one of his houses."

"They can't do a thing like that!" Benny said wildly. "By God! I won't let them do it!" He got to his feet.

Jay said, "You don't understand. You've got to take it. There's nothing we can do. Now listen; they know I'm on to their racket, so what do they do? I've got to go to New York to cover the Tammany Hall trial. That's just getting me out of the way. I've got no come-back. I gotta do it. If I turn it down I'm on the black list, and I can't afford to be on that."

Benny said thickly, "And what am I supposed to do? Sit around and let them get away with it?"

"If I hadn't told you, you wouldn't have done anything. I've got no proof of all this. No, you've got to wait. Go and see Grantham and try and sell him some trucks. Try and find out who's taken over the organization. Maybe it is Grantham, but somehow I can't see him holding a job of work down as big as that. Anyway, snoop around. Don't start anything. Just snoop. When I get back I'm goin' to go after this business with both hands."

Benny said, "If you think I'm going to sit around while Sadie's in those bastards' hands you're crazy. I'm going right over and split Grantham open."

"You sucker," Jay said. "How far will that get you? If you make it too hot you'll ran into a belly-load of slugs. Will that help Sadie? No, there's only one way of handling this, and that's by taking it slow. We can't help her now. Whatever's happened to her or is going to happen to her we can't stop. The cops won't listen to you. You can't force your way in twenty brothels and search for her. You've got to consider she's dead. Do you understand? You're not looking for her, you're avenging her."

He got to his feet and went to the door. "I've got to catch my train. Stick around, Perminger, and take it."

Benny sat in the chair and watched him go. His hands gripped the chair-arms until his knuckles showed white. He began to swear slowly and obscenely, using words that he never spoke aloud. Then quite suddenly he put his hands over his face and began to cry.

21

June 6th, 3 p.m.

Sadie opened her eyes as the door swung open. She had fallen into an exhausted sleep and her dreams had been terrifying. She sat up on the bed, her hand going to her mouth and her eyes dark with fear.

Fan came in and shut the door behind her. The silk wrap

that she wore outlined her full figure. There was no mistaking what she was.

Sadie caught her breath when she saw her. Her mouth was so dry that she couldn't say anything.

"Take it easy," Fan said, leaning against the door; "I've been told to have a little talk with you."

Still Sadie couldn't say anything. She continued to stare at her with growing horror.

Fan said crossly, "Don't look at me like that. You're givin' me the heebies. Relax, sister."

"Who are you?" Sadie managed to get out.

"What does it matter?" Fan asked, giving a hard little smile. "You worry about yourself. You're in a spot."

"Where am I? What does all this mean?"

Fan came over to the bed and sat down. "I've got to talk to you," she said. "Don't think I want to, but when I'm told to do anythin' in this joint it's easier to do it than to kick. The old cow downstairs has sent me up to scare you. Well, I ain't goin' to. I'm goin' to tell you what'll be good for you, and what you ought to do."

Sadie said, "But tell me where I am."

"Can't you guess?" Fan said bitterly. "Take a look at me? What do you think I am—a nun?"

Sadie felt herself go suddenly very cold. She flinched away from Fan.

"Skip it, sister," Fan said roughly. "You don't have to take it that way. You're in the same boat as me. I don't know why they've picked on you, but they're goin' to put you through it. If you take my advice you'll do as you're told and get off lightly."

Sadie looked at her in horror.

"There's a nigger who runs this house. She's tough. Make no mistake about it. She's had dozens of girls like you through her hands. Some of them stuck it for a hell of a long time. They wouldn't do what she wanted. But they did in the end. You'll do it too. Maybe you don't think you will, but you will."

Sadie said, "Get me out of here. I'll give you anything if you'll get me out of here."

"Skip it. No amount of that talk will help. I can't do anythin' for you. All I can tell you is what'll come to you if you buck."

Sadie controlled her nerves with a great effort. "They won't make me do that," she said fiercely. "They'll have to kill me first. I won't!"

Fan took a packet of cigarettes from her pocket. "Have one?" she said, shaking two out on the sheet.

Sadie didn't even look at them. "If you won't help me, then I want to see someone else," she said. "You can't do this sort of thing in this country and get away with it."

Fan lit a cigarette and put the odd one back in the packet. "Don't be a sap," she said. "A kid like you don't know anythin'. Listen, sister, have you ever been whipped?"

Sadie flushed hotly. "What's that got to do with it?"

"You tell me. Have you?"

"Of course I haven't. Why should I be?"

"Well, I have." Fan said grimly. "And believe me it ain't pleasant. When Carrie comes up she'll explain what she wants done. You'll say yes or no. If it's yes, then you'll be okay; if it's no—Gawd help you. She'll tie you to that bed and she'll whip you. She'll whip you until you say yes. Don't think she'll get tired of it—she won't. She'll whip you every hour of the day until you can't take any more of it. And when she's broken you you'll be doin' what you said no to in the first place."

Sadie said quietly, "She can do anythin' she likes to me—but I'll never agree."

Fan sighed. "It's always the same," she said. "My God, I'm sick of all this! She sends me up to talk you kids into being sensible, but you all say the same. You all think you've got enough guts to take it and in the end you give way. Why don't you be sensible? What the hell's the use of being bashed about, losing your nice skin, just because you ain't got the brains to know when you're sunk?"

Sadie shook her head. "Nothin' you can say will make any difference," she said.

"Carrie distrusts a dame she has had to beat into submission. She makes sure that she'll stick when she finally gives in. There won't be much kick-back coming from you. Can't you see this is the one time you can't beat the rap? You can't get away. Carrie's got everything the way she wants it. She won't have any mercy on you. I'm tellin' you. Use your nut and give in right away. It'll be tough, but it ain't goin' to be the hell you'll make for yourself if you try and stick it. I've said my little bit. It's up to you. She'll be up in a while. Think it over." She got off the bed.

Sadie beat her to it. She darted across the room, wrenched open the door and ran into the passage. Fan grimaced. She made no attempt to intercept her.

Sadie could see a flight of stairs at the end of the passage. Blindly she ran towards them. Halfway down the stairs she became aware that someone was waiting for her at the bottom. She brought herself up with a jerk.

Carrie, her flat face expressionless, looked up at her. "Go back to your room," she said harshly.

Sadie didn't move. Her heart pounded against her side. She felt as if she had suddenly become involved in a horrible nightmare.

"Go back to your room," Carrie repeated.

Sadie retreated one step up. Then, realizing that this would be her one chance of escape, she said, "You've got to let me go—do you hear? You can't do this to me."

Carrie began to climb the stairs slowly. Her big mouth gaped in a grin. "Go on back," she said. "I'm comin' to talk to you. Look what I've got for you."

Sadie saw she was holding a thin length of whalebone in her hand. She caught her breath and turned to run up the stairs. A powerfully built negro was standing at the head of the stairs, blocking her escape. He grinned at her; his thick lips seemed to split his face in half.

Paralysed with terror, Sadie turned again. Carrie was right on her. She said, "Go to your room."

Sadie suddenly clutched her head between her hands and began to scream. Her screams resounded against the walls.

The negro ran down the few stairs and grabbed her. She nearly went mad with terror as his great damp hands closed on her.

"Get her upstairs—quick!" Carrie said angrily. "She'll disturb my people."

The negro, grinning broadly, carried Sadie up the stairs. Her arms and legs banged against the sides of the wall as he carried her. She twisted and struggled frantically, but the grip round her arms and thighs was immovable. She continued to scream until she heard the door shut with a thud, and then she went limp.

Carrie said, "She doesn't know anythin' yet. Put her on the bed, Joe."

The negro lowered her on to the bed and stood away. His face beamed. Sadie half lay, half crouched, looking at Carrie.

The mulatto stood, her big hands hanging loosely at her sides and her big eyes blazing with a curious animal expression. "My girls know how to behave themselves in this house," she said. "You better learn."

Sadie had lost her fear. She was nearly suffocating with rage. Her Southern blood had revolted at the touch of the negro. She said furiously, "You'll pay for this! How dare you touch me!... How dare you touch me!"

Carrie glanced at the negro. "All right, Joe. Fix her up for me."

The negro shuffled across the room. Sadie could see little red tints in his eyes as he came towards her. She said wildly, shrinking back on the bed, "Don't touch me!" And then he was on her. The horrible rancid nigger smell of him sickened her, and she struck at him twice before he pinned her hands. He muttered, "She'll sure take the hide off you for this, baby," and twisting her arms, he turned her over on her face. His knee rammed down between her shoulders and she felt her hands being fixed to the bedposts.

Sobbing with rage, she kicked and twisted, moving the bed half across the room. One of her ankles was seized and fastened to the lower bedpost. She kicked wildly with her free leg and she felt a jar as she caught the negro in his chest. He grunted, grabbed the flaying leg and fastened that too. Then he got off the bed and looked at Carrie with a little smirk.

Sadie pulled and strained on the cords that held her, but they only bit further into her flesh. She was securely tied, face down on the bed.

Then she gave herself up for lost. No one would come at the last moment and save her from this horror. She knew that she would not wake up to find that it had only been some strange and horrible nightmare. It was real and it was happening to her. And when the negro began to rip the clothes off her back she screamed like a terrified child.

PART TWO

1

August 16th, 10.15 p.m.

Little Joe walked into the pool-room at the corner of 29th Street. He was pleasantly conscious of the sudden hush that greeted his entrance. Even the guys at the tables paused in their game and looked at him with interest.

He was something to look at now. His suit was heavily padded at the shoulders and its colour compelled a second glance. When Little Joe first saw it hanging in a window of a Jewish tailor his mouth watered. He'd never seen a suit quite like it. He knew there couldn't be another on the streets that came anywhere near it, so he went inside and bought it. Also he was persuaded to buy a pair of yellow shoes, a bowler hat that only just fitted him and a necktie that, to say the least, was completely surrealist. The barman wiped down the counter and smiled at him. "Why, Joe," he said, "you're lookin' pretty good tonight."

Little Joe adjusted his bowler. "Like it?" he said. "I bet you ain't seen anythin' quite like this, huh?"

The barman said truthfully he hadn't. His tone was so dubious that Little Joe scowled. "Ain't nothin' the matter with it, is there?" he said. "I gave a heap of jack for this outfit."

The barman told him hastily that it was swell.

Little Joe relaxed a trifle. "Gimme some Scotch," he said. "Not every guy could wear a suit like this," he went on, pouring out a liberal shot; "you gotta have somethin' to get away with it."

A big fat guy, who had been playing snooker over the other side of the room, suddenly laid down his cue and came over. He owned a bunch of taxi-cabs that beat up a good business in the lower East side of the town. His name was Spade. Little Joe knew him well enough to nod to.

Spade was looking worried. When he got close to Little Joe

he said, "I've been wantin' to talk to you, buddy. Come over to the table, will you?"

Little Joe followed him to a corner of the room and sat down.

"Well, what is it?" he asked, taking off his hat and brushing it carefully with his sleeve. "What do you want to see me about?"

Spade rubbed his hand over his fat features and shook his head. He certainly looked as if he was in a lot of trouble. "What's come over the town, Joe?" he said.

Little Joe stared at him. "What the hell are you talkin' about?"

Spade fingered his glass. "Where've the girls got to?"

Little Joe was non-committal. "What girls?" he asked.

Spade shook his head again. "You know. There ain't a floosie poundin' a beat this side of 27th Street. A couple of months ago you couldn't take a step without fallin' over them. Well, where've they gone?"

Little Joe grinned. "Can't you find any comfort?"

"It ain't that," Spade said. "It's ruinin' my business. I've gotta find out what's wrong."

"What do you mean—ruinin' your business?"

"What I say. When one of those floosie's found a sucker she took one of my cabs. My cabs were kept mighty busy doin' that business—now it's all gone."

Little Joe looked perplexed. He hadn't thought of it in that light. Spade was a member of the Hack Drivers Union and he'd got a certain amount of political influence.

"What makes you think I know anythin' about it?" he said cautiously.

"I use my eyes and my ears. They said Raven's at the back of the vice ring now. I know you've done a lot for Raven. You're in the dough now. Anyone can see that by the fancy uniform you're wearin'—"

"Let me tell you," Little Joe said heatedly, "this suit cost me—"

"Skip it," Spade said roughly. "What's goin' on?"

Little Joe hesitated. "Maybe the girls've got scared," he said at last.

"If they've got scared, someone's scarin' them. You'd better lay off, Joe, an' you can tell Raven to lay off too. No one's goin' to bust up my business without hearin' from me."

"Take it easy," Little Joe said hastily. "I don't know a thing about it—honest. I'll have a word with Raven. I can't promise anythin'. He's a hard guy."

Spade got to his feet. "So am I," he said shortly. "Tell him that, too."

Little Joe watched him walk across the room and resume his game. He took a little splinter of wood from his pocket and began to explore his teeth thoughtfully. Then he got up and walked out into the dark night again.

He knew Spade was a dangerous guy to cross. He'd got a lot of pull and he might make things difficult for them. Well, anyway, that was Raven's look-out. He wasn't paid to strain his brains.

He made his way in the direction of St. Louis Hotel. The fact that he had now plenty of dough did not allow him to take a taxi. He had been so long used to being short that he could not bring himself to throw money away on unnecessary luxuries.

It was a hot night, dark and moonless, and Little Joe moved slowly, his eyes searching the shadows. At the head of the street he noticed a woman step out of the darkness and stop a guy who was hurrying towards the main street. The guy paused, then waved his hand impatiently and went on.

Little Joe grinned. Some dame was ignoring the warning he had circulated through the bookers. He put his hand in his pocket and his fingers touched the little bottle he always carried around with him. He took the bottle out and carefully removed the glass stopper. He put the glass stopper in a small metal box. Then, holding the bottle between two fingers, he sauntered slowly towards the woman.

As he drew near he could see she was scared. She was watching him as he came on. He slowed down and looked at her, his free hand adjusting his tie.

She must have thought he was all right, because she smiled at him. He could see her now. She was only quite a kid. She looked a little shabby, but she wasn't a bad looker. Her professional smile wasn't very gay.

He said, "I bet you're a naughty girl."

She came close to him. "Do you want a naughty girl?" she said, smiling with her mouth only. "I've got a little place just round the corner."

"What's the big idea?" Little Joe asked. "I've walked two blocks an' you're the first girl I've met."

He saw the little twitch of panic at her mouth. "I—I don't know," she said. "Anyway, you've found me—"

"Yeah, I've found you all right. Maybe the other girls think it healthier to stay at home," Little Joe said, tossing the vitriol into her face. He heard the little hiss as the acid travelled through the air. Then she began to scream horribly.

Little Joe broke into a run. He knew the district very well, and by doubling down an alley and then a side street he reached the St. Louis very quickly.

Raven would never let any of his mob come in through the front entrance. They all came in by the staff door. He knew that there'd be a lot of trouble from the hotel if Little Joe kept coming in and out in that suit of his.

Little Joe rode up in the small elevator, very pleased with himself. How he dealt with that floosie would get around. The girls would think twice before coming out. He rapped on Raven's door, and Maltz let him in.

"Boss in?"

Maltz nodded. "Yeah," he said in a bored voice; "he's playin' with his toys."

Little Joe grinned. "I'll get his mind on to somethin' else," he said, moving towards the big double doors at the end of the passage.

"Not a chance. That guy's very busy right now."

Little Joe opened the doors and stepped quietly into the big room.

Raven had spread himself. The suite at the St. Louis was costing him plenty, but it did him a lot of good. It had increased his own confidence.

He lay on the floor in a red silk dressing-gown. All around him was a complicated network of railway lines. Miniature stations, signals, buffers, engine-sheds and the like surrounded him. Trains, dragging long lines of carriages, flashed over points and rattled over the gleaming metal track. They disappeared beneath furniture, only to reappear again, running in an endless circle.

He lay there, his hands on a master switch, controlling the

current that sent the trains forward. A limp cigarette hung from his thin lips, and his eyes were cloudy and intent on the fast-moving little trains.

"What is it?" he said suddenly. "One of these days you're goin' to collect a handful of slugs if yon sneak up on me like this."

Little Joe grinned nervously. "Sure, boss," he said.

Reluctantly Raven closed the switch, bringing the trains to a standstill. He rolled over a little on his side so that he could look at Joe. "Nice outfit, ain't it?" he said with a proud smile.

"Yeah." Joe wasn't very interested. "It's all right."

Raven turned back again and set the trains in motion. "Well, what is it?"

"A floosie on 7th Street was peddling. I gave her a little tonic."

Raven grunted. "You gotta watch those dames," he said. "Another month an' we'll have it where we want it."

"Before that, boss," Little Joe said, sitting on the arm of a big overstuffed chair. "The guys are yappin' like hell now."

Raven directed a train to a station and threw the switch. He leant forward to uncouple it. "Always wanted an outfit like this when I was a lad," he said. "I never got anythin' when I was a kid." His voice was suddenly very bitter.

Joe didn't say anything.

Raven started a complicated move of shunting the train to the engine-house. Little Joe couldn't understand why he didn't just lift the train off the track and put it in the shed. He thought it would save a lot of time.

"Well, what is it?" Raven repeated for the third time.

"Spade's bellyachin'."

"So what?"

"He says we're ruinin' his taxi business."

Raven at last got the engine in the shed. "That's too bad," he said, stubbing out his cigarette in an ash-tray by his side. Then, as an afterthought, he said, "Are we?"

"His taxis take the floosies to their joints," Little Joe explained.

Raven paused and thought. "I don't want trouble with Spade," he said at last. "He's a tough egg, ain't he?"

"You bet he is," Little Joe said.

Raven began to unload some tiny milk churns on to the platform. "I'll get Lefty to take care of him," he said. "We ain't had any shootin' in the town yet, have we?"

Little Joe looked worried. "Gee!" he said. "We don't want to shoot Spade."

"Nice to hear your views," Raven said, recoupling the line of trucks; "I'll make a note of that."

Little Joe shifted uneasily. "You're the boss," he said hastily.

"Sure." Raven turned the switch and the trains began to move slowly along the track.

Little Joe waited for a little while, and as Raven continued to ignore him he went out, closing the door softly behind him.

Raven turned his head and looked at the closed door. A cold, far-away look came into his eyes. "So we don't want to shoot Spade?" he said softly. "These guys are gettin' soft."

2

August 17th, 11.25 a.m.

When Grantham rang the bell the negro doorman let him in.

Grantham was looking old and tired. He asked for Carrie in a voice tight with nerves.

Joe showed him into a little reception-room. "She'll be right down, boss," he said. His big eyes searched Grantham's face questioningly, but Grantham turned away and felt for his cigarette-case.

When Carrie came in she found him pacing up and down the room, smoking furiously. She shut the door. "What's the matter?" she asked abruptly. She always liked to get straight to the point.

Grantham motioned her to a chair. "Things ain't goin' right," he said shortly. "I don't know what the hell Raven's playin' at."

Carrie rested her big hands on her knees. "He's a bad man," she said. "It was wrong to let him take over."

Grantham threw away his cigarette impatiently. "Don't go over that again!" he snapped. "I couldn't stop him. He's playin' some deep game, and I don't know what's at the back of it."

Carrie shook her head. "One of his hoods threw vitriol over a hustler yesterday. All the girls are too scared to work. It's crazy, Grantham. Most of the business is done on the streets. It's only a certain class that come to the houses."

Grantham nodded. "We're losin' money," he said. "I'm goin' along right now to have it out with him. Before I see him I wanted to know about the Perminger girl. She all right?"

Carrie smiled. "Sure she's all right."

Grantham stroked his jaw with a hand that shook a little. "That dame may be very useful to us if Raven doesn't behave," he said. "You understand that, don't you?"

Carrie nodded.

"Where is she?"

"Upstairs. Do you want to see her?"

Grantham hesitated, then he stood up. "No. It's better not for me to see her yet. I'm relyin' on you, Carrie. You've got to keep her the way we want her—don't forget that."

"It's all right."

"He hasn't been here, has he?"

"I haven't seen him. Lefty's been in. He looked the girls over and took all their names."

Grantham's eyes snapped. "Did he see the Perminger dame?"

Carrie nodded. "Sure. He went all over the house. He came in unexpected. I couldn't get her out of the way."

"Did he speak to her?"

"He spoke to them all."

"Did she behave all right?"

"I was right behind her." Carrie gave a cruel little smile. "He just thought she was one of the girls."

"You're sure? She didn't do or say anythin' that'd give a guy like Lefty ideas?"

"It was all right, I tell you," Carrie said a little shortly.

Grantham sighed. "I'm tippin' you, Carrie. If Raven knew about this, he'd finish both of us."

Carrie shrugged a little. "Maybe it'd be better to get rid of her," she said. "It's a pity. She's a nice bit of meat."

Grantham suddenly stiffened. "You ain't usin' her?"

"Why not? She uses food, don't she? I don't have dead

heads around here."

"You mean you've hired her out?"

"Only to the guys who I can trust. She doesn't know who's a stranger or not. If she opens her mouth she'll get another lickin'. You'd be surprised how she hates a lickin'." Carrie laughed.

Grantham shook his head. "I don't like it," he said.

"I know what's right," Carrie returned. "She's lost all her starch now—that was the only way to make her lose it."

"All right, I'll leave it to you," Grantham said, opening the door. "I'll go and see Raven."

When he had gone Carrie went upstairs. She went into the big reception-room, where the girls were getting ready for the evening's work.

Lulu was painting her nails. Julie and Andree were doing some limbering-up exercises. Fan, her face screwed up with concentration and the tip of her tongue protruding, was writing a letter. In the far corner of the room Sadie sat in a yellow wrap, reading the newspaper.

They all looked up when Carrie came in. Fan sneered and returned to her letter. Carrie was aware of the long look of hatred that she got from Sadie. That didn't worry her any.

She said, "You—I want you."

Sadie put down the newspaper and got to her feet. Her face was now a hard, cold mask. "What is it?"

"Come on out here. I want to talk to you."

They went out together. Sadie followed Carrie into her own little room.

"You hate me, don't you?" Carrie said with a little grin. "Well, that's all right. But you'd hate the guy who got you here a damn sight more, wouldn't you?"

Sadie stood by the door. She didn't say anything.

Carrie said, "Do you know why you're here?"

Still Sadie didn't say anything. Her eyes smouldered with bitter hatred for the mulatto.

"You've seen too much," Carrie told her. "You saw the guy who killed Mendetta."

Sadie flinched.

"Yeah," Carrie went on, "he's a bad guy. He runs this house. One of these days, baby, you're goin' to get a chance of puttin' that guy where you want him. That'll make you happy, won't it?"

Sadie clenched her fists. "One of these days," she said, "I'm goin' to even the score out all round. You don't think you can get away with this for ever. You've turned me into one of these women because I haven't got the guts to fight you, but I'm not forgetting. Make no mistake about that."

Carrie laughed. "Go back to your room. You've got to work tonight."

Sadie went out silently.

3

August 17th, 10.30 p.m.

Lefty walked softly down the dark alley, his hands in his coat pockets, his hat drawn well over his eyes, and a cigarette glowed in the darkness, moving up and down as he shifted it in his mouth.

Spade's big garage ran half the block, and Lefty was walking down the alley that ran immediately behind it. As he came to a lighted window he threw his cigarette away. Stretching up, he took one quick look into the room, saw Spade sitting there checking a ledger, and grinned.

He went on until he came to the back door and let himself in. He moved quietly down the dark passage. Faintly he could hear the crews in the garage washing the cabs down. He could hear the murmur of voices and an occasional laugh.

He knocked gently on Spade's office door and went in. Spade looked up sharply. His face cleared when he saw Lefty. "Come in," he said. "Raven sent you?"

Lefty shut the door softly. "Yeah," he said. "You got a little trouble, ain't you?"

"Sit down. I'm glad you've come. It's time we had a talk. Why didn't Raven come himself?"

"He's busy," Lefty said, still standing. "You know a lot, don't you?"

Spade shrugged. "You mean about Raven? Why, sure. It's my job to know things. Raven's been behind Grantham since Mendetta was bumped. I know that too."

Lefty nodded. "Bright boy," he said. "What else do you know?"

Spade reached for a pipe and began to load it. "I know, for some reason or other, Raven's driven the girls off the streets. It ain't that he wants a clean town. Raven ain't that sort of a guy. He's done it for something that'll fill his pockets, but I don't like it."

"Too bad," Lefty said, and smiled mirthlessly.

Spade struck a match and for a moment his big face was hidden behind blue smoke. "I want to know why," he said.

"You know a lot. Why don't you find out?"

"If you're goin' to take that angle, I will," Spade snapped, his face darkening. "Listen, Lefty, this isn't the way to take it. I'm willin' to work with you boys, but I can't let you ruin my trade. What the hell is all this about? Can't you see you ain't doin' yourselves any good clearin' the streets like this?"

"Raven thinks it's a grand idea."

"Well, I don't. I'm tellin' you it's gotta stop." Spade thumped his fist on the desk. "I thought you'd come along to talk business."

Lefty shook his head. "Nope, we can't help you, buddy. The girls stay off the streets."

Spade nodded. "Okay," he said. "Then you can't blame me if it gets tough for you boys. I ain't givin' way on it. I can't afford to. I'll give you till next week. If the girls ain't workin' then I'll have to start somethin'."

Lefty took a blunt-nose automatic from his pocket. "You'll just be a big smell in the ground, buddy," he said evenly. "Raven sends this with his love."

The automatic cracked once. Spade half rose from his chair. A big blot of blood suddenly appeared between his eyes. He spread out his hands and then fell forward over the desk.

Lefty ran over to the window, threw it up and climbed into the dark alley. He ran very quickly to the car parked at the end of the alley. Maltz swung the door open for him and Little Joe started the car rolling. Long before Spade had been found the car was out of sight.

Maltz said, "Did you get him?"

"Sure. He went out like a light. Raven was right. He knew too much," Lefty said.

Little Joe said uneasily, "There'll be a hell of a row about this."

"Aw, shut up!" Lefty snarled. "It's time we got tough in this burg. I've been fed up just hangin' around chasin' dames off the street."

"Where the hell's it goin' to get us?" Little Joe said, heading towards the St. Louis Hotel. "Ain't we got enough dough?"

Maltz said very softly, "Turnin' yellow, Joe?"

Little Joe said hastily, "No. I was just wonderin'."

"Well, don't wonder, then."

They drove the rest of the way in silence.

Raven was waiting for them. His thin, wolfish face was hard and set as they came in. "Well?" he said.

Lefty nodded. "It's okay," he said. "Nobody saw me."

Raven took a turn up and down the room. "We're goin' to get goin' now," he said. "Grantham's been in. He's yellin' about bad business. I want you and Maltz to come with me. We're goin' to look Mendetta's houses over."

Lefty nodded. "I've got the list of dames in each house," he said. "Shall I bring it along?"

"Of course." Raven went to the door. "Let's go."

In the car Lefty said, "Carrie's house is the best one."

Raven nodded. "We'll go there."

When they ran up the steps the negro Joe thought they were the cops. He rang the alarm bell. Carrie appeared on the scene, her eyes snapping with fury. When she saw Lefty she ran towards him. "What the hell's this?" she said angrily. "Do you want to ruin my business?"

Lefty pushed her on one side. "Keep your chest in place," he said. "The big shot's come to look the joint over."

Carrie turned quickly. She had never seen Raven, although she had heard a lot about him. She said, "You can't come in here. I've got my customers to think of. The girls are busy."

Raven looked her up and down. "Clear all your customers out," he said shortly; "I want to look the girls over. Come on, jump to it."

Carrie said, "Like hell I will. You come in the morning."

Raven looked at Maltz, who swung his fist, hitting Carrie very hard on the side of her jaw. She went down in a heap on the floor.

"You heard me the first time, nigger," Raven said.

Carrie got slowly to her feet. A livid mark showed on her yellow skin. She turned and went away slowly.

Raven said, "The girls I select will be taken to Franky's place. The other girls can pack up and get out. Do you understand that?"

Maltz nodded. He went to the front door and signalled.

A large van drew up to the kerb and four men got out. They stood waiting.

It was early. There were only three clients in the house. They came downstairs, looking scared.

Raven opened the door for them. "It's all right," he said with his crooked grin. "Just checkin' up. You boys can get off home."

They looked at him furtively and left quickly. Carrie stood at the bottom of the stairs, waiting.

Raven nodded at her. "Bring all your girls down here fast," he said.

Carrie went upstairs again. A few minutes later she came down, followed by seven lightly clad girls.

Raven went into the reception-room. "Come in here," he said.

The girls all looked at Carrie, who was nearly speechless with rage. "Go on in. Didn't you hear him?" she snarled.

The girls went into the room and stood staring at Raven. Lulu fluffed up her hair. "Take me, darlin'," she said. "I'll show you some tricks."

The other girls giggled.

Raven said, "Shut up!" Then he turned to Maltz. "Are they all here?"

Maltz took out his list and checked the numbers. "One ain't," he said briefly.

Raven looked over at Carrie. "I said all of them."

Carrie hesitated a moment, then went upstairs again. After a few minutes Sadie followed her down.

Raven's eyes lit up a little when he saw her. This one was good, he told himself. When he looked at her he saw her go suddenly very white and her step falter. Carrie took her arm and shoved her forward. She muttered something that Raven didn't hear. He made a mental note to look into this. Sadie stood beside the other girls, her dark eyes big with fear, gazing steadily at Raven. It made him a little uncomfortable.

He looked away from her. "I've got somethin' to say to you girls," he said abruptly. "I'm Raven. I run this racket. There's goin' to be some changes. Get into a line, you girls. Snap to it!"

A little buzz filled the room as the girls stared at him. Maltz stepped forward. "Quiet," he said loudly. "Get into a line. Go on, damn you, get into a line!"

They slowly formed into a line and stood giggling and nudging each other.

Raven lit a cigarette. "Take your things off. All of 'em. Your stockings as well."

"I ain't takin' orders from a bum like that. What's the game, Carrie?" Lulu shrilled.

Raven made a little sign to Maltz. Maltz stepped forward and dragged Lulu out of the line. He slapped her twice across her face with his open palm, before she could dodge, and then he shoved her back into the line again.

She was so dazed by the heavy blows she could only rock on her heels, blinking away the tears that had started to her eyes.

Raven said, "The next dame who cracks wise will get a boot. Get undressed."

Muttering angrily, the girls took off their things. Raven stood by watching them. "Now stand still and let me look at you."

Sadie was the only one who didn't undress. Maltz took a step towards her, but Raven stopped him. He looked the girls over as if he were inspecting cattle. Then he grunted: "They're all right. Take the lot."

Little Joe, who was standing by the doorway with a large embarrassed grin on his face, clapped his hands. "Break it up, girls," he said. "Get dressed quick. We're goin' for a ride."

Raven beckoned to Maltz. "What's that dame's name?" he asked, pointing to Sadie.

Maltz consulted his list and then told him.

Raven nodded. "Take her to the St. Louis. I want to talk to her. Lock her up. See she doesn't start anythin', an' keep your hands off her."

Maltz looked hurt. "Gee!" he said. "I could use a honey like that."

"If you touch her, I'll fix you," Raven snarled. "Get on with it." He turned to Carrie. "Get all these girls upstairs. Get 'em dressed to go out. Tell 'em to bring stuff for a night and you come yourself. Hurry."

Carrie opened her mouth to say something, but thought better of it. She shepherded the girls out of the room.

Upstairs, she turned on Sadie. "You're not to tell that guy you know him," she said. "Do you understand? When the time's right, then you can fix him... not before."

Sadie didn't say anything.

Carrie went on: "If you blow the gaff I'll come after you. I'll find you okay. Then I'll do things to you until you wish you were dead. I mean that."

Sadie flinched away from her and continued to dress. The other girls were puzzled and angry. All their questions were met with a stony stare from Carrie. All she would say was, "He's the boss—ask him."

Downstairs, Raven jerked his head to Lefty. "Come on, we've got a lotta houses to look at before we sleep. These guys will look after the girls. Watch that pippin, Maltz."

Maltz nodded. "You bet," he said sourly. "I'll watch her."

Raven and Lefty went out and drove away.

Little Joe came up to Maltz. "This racket's gettin' interestin', ain't it?" he said. "That's the best bit of striptease I've seen for a long time."

Maltz ignored him.

4

August 18th, 2.10 a.m.

Raven walked into the lobby of the St. Louis Hotel, followed by Little Joe and Lefty. He went immediately to the elevator which took him up to his suite.

Little Joe leant against the wall of the cage, his eyes half closed and a look of tired satisfaction softening the lines of his face. "I ain't seen so many floosies all at one time in my life," he said. "Gee! Some of them were hot numbers."

Lefty shrugged. "So much meat to me," he said. "I've got no

use for it when it's tossed at me like that."

"Shut up, you two!" Raven said savagely. He had had a trying evening, but the first step of his scheme was successfully launched.

They went into the suite. Maltz was sitting in a large chair, dozing. He started up as they came in.

Raven looked at him hard. "She all right?"

Maltz rubbed his eyes. "Yeah," he said; "she's sleepin' in there."

Raven nodded and sat down. He tossed his hat on to the table. "Get me a drink, one of you," he said, lighting a cigarette.

Little Joe went over to the wall cupboard and began to fix drinks.

Raven stretched. "Right now," he said, "there ain't a girl hustling in this town." He said it with great satisfaction. "Over at Franky's we've got a hundred and forty picked hustlers. The rest of the stuff is finished. Tomorrow we're calling a meeting of bookers. I'm goin' to explain what they've got to do. In another week we'll reopen the houses. Then we'll make money."

Maltz took a whisky from Little Joe. "What are the bookers supposed to do?"

"They're goin' to work for a change," Raven said grimly. "We've got twenty houses. Each house can take thirty hustlers. We've got a hundred and forty already. They got to get me four hundred and sixty new girls. They've got to get them fast. I've been working this out. We can get girls from Kansas City, Jefferson City, Denver, Springfields, and Cleveland. Once I get these houses started we'll organize houses in these towns as well. In every case we're goin' to secure a monopoly. Hustlers are not to work on the streets. We can't check on their earnings if they do. This'll take time. It's goin' to be big. The bookers will have to organize themselves and have a clearing-post. This can be at Sedalia. I don't care how they get the stuff. That's their look-out. The girls will only stay at one house for a week, then they'll be moved on to another house. Grantham's got to do some work. I'm takin' him out of the 22nd. Any guy can run that joint. Grantham's got brains, but he's lazy. You three guys have got to get busy too. Give me two months and you'll all be makin' more dough than you'll know what to do with."

Little Joe's face fell. Actually he was already getting more money than he knew how to spend.

Raven finished his drink and stood up. "Tomorrow you guys beat up the bookers and take them along to Franky's. We'll have a general meeting and then I'll explain to the girls what's comin' to them. Get some of the boys. I want the tough ones. Tell 'em to bring clubs. We might have a little trouble with some of those dames."

The three nodded and left him.

Raven wandered up and down the room, thinking. He knew he would have to play his game very carefully. It was worth the risks. If he slipped up on the Mann Act he was sunk.

He tossed his cigarette away and went into the bathroom to wash his hands. He didn't feel like sleep. His brain was too active. Quietly he crossed the room and opened the door of the spare bedroom. His hand reached out and groped for the light switch.

Sadie said out of the darkness, "Who is it?" Her voice sounded husky with fear.

Raven turned on the light.

She sat up, holding the sheet close to her chin. Her eyes looked very dark and big and her face was the colour of chalk.

Raven came and leant over the bedrail. "I want to talk to you," he said quietly.

There was a long pause, then he went on, "How long have you been hustlin'?"

She didn't say anything.

He came round and sat on the bed. "If you don't answer my questions I'll hurt you," he said. "How long?"

She looked at the thin face, the cold, merciless eyes and the paper-thin lips. She said, "I was forced into this two months ago."

"Why?"

"I don't know."

"Why didn't Carrie want me to see you?"

"I don't know."

Raven said, "Get out of bed and take that thing off."

Sadie shook her head wildly. "No..." she said, clinging to the sheet. "Leave me alone."

"Do it," Raven said.

"No. You're not touchin' me. I'll scream—I'll scream...."

Raven hit her on the side of her jaw very hard. Her head snapped back and she went limp, falling against the top of the bed with a little thud.

He got off the bed, went into the other room and found some cord. He came back again, stripped off the sheet, turned her over on her face and tied her hands behind her. He turned her again and gagged her with her stockings that hung over the bedrail. Then he fastened her ankles securely to each of the bedposts. By the time he had finished she had recovered from the blow. Her eyes pleaded, but he didn't look at her.

He went out and came back after a few minutes with a small bottle containing some colourless fluid. He sat down beside her on the bed. "After tonight you'll do anything that I tell you without hesitation. I ain't got time to persuade you. I like a dame to obey. You'll obey after this."

He took the cork out of the bottle and, bending over her shrinking body, poured the fluid on to her nightdress, low down.

She jerked as the cold fluid ran down her body. A strong smell of turpentine filled the room. Raven got up and replaced the cork. "It'll take a couple of weeks to get over this," he said with a little grin. "But I can wait. I shan't have to do it again."

She lay very still, a puzzled look in her eyes. She couldn't understand why he had done this. She felt nothing, only the cold wetness on her skin. She could understand pain, she could understand beating, but this defeated her.

He made sure that her bonds were tight, testing the knots carefully. He adjusted the gag and then he straightened.

The puzzled look in her eyes suddenly gave way to fear. The fluid began to penetrate. She twisted this way and that as the horrible burning sensation began to grow.

Raven nodded. "I'll see you in the morning," he said, turning out the light, and went away, leaving her writhing in the heavy darkness.

5

September 7th, 2.20 p.m.

When Special Prosecutor Dewey said, "Don't you remember any testimony about Hines and the poultry racket there by him?" Jay Ellinger dropped his pencil and sat back with a gasp.

Hines's defender, Stryker, was already on his feet, shouting, "I demand a mistrial. Your Honour! Your Honour! I demand a mistrial!"

Ellinger whispered to the Tribune reporter, "It's over. They've been waitin' for a loophole like this."

The Tribune reporter shook his head. "Naw," he said, "they'll go on. This goddamn' trial will last for years."

But Ellinger knew in his bones that Dewey had made just that one little slip that would give the Judge the chance of getting Hines freed. Although the trial dragged on over the week-end, by Monday everyone knew that Dewey's tremendous work of bringing Hines to trial had to be started all over again.

Ellinger got his copy off and then immediately caught a train back to East St. Louis. He was determined to resign before he could be sent on some other job that would keep him from the work he had been impatiently waiting to tackle.

Since he had been away he hadn't heard one word from Benny. He had been so busy attending the Hines trial that he had not been able to check up with the home town news. Now, as he stepped out of the train, he could hardly contain his patience to get started.

He took a taxi to the Banner offices and went immediately to see Henry.

He burst into the office. Henry gaped at him. "What the hell are you doin' here?" he snapped. "I want—"

"Save it," Jay said quickly; "I'm through. I quit. I resign.... Get it?"

Henry relaxed in his chair. "Wait a minute," he said. "You gone crazy?"

Jay sat down. "No," he said, "I'm just through. I thought I'd get that in before you gave me another little job out of town.

Poison ain't keeping me muzzled any more, Henry. I'm working on my own for a while."

Henry sighed. "Okay," he said, "I'll tell him."

"Now listen, Chief, tell me what's been goin' on. Anythin' new on the Mendetta angle?"

Henry lit a cigar. "Plenty," he said briefly. "Vice's been organized on a big scale here. From reports that I hear, whoever it is who's running the game is doing it on a real money-making scheme. He's got the monopoly here. The girls have been driven off the streets. You've never seen anything like it. You won't find one single girl poundin' a beat. Even the cops couldn't clean up a town as this guy's done. But he's got houses everywhere. At his own prices. The rake-off must be colossal."

"Who is it?"

Henry shrugged. "They say it's Grantham. He's payin' all the bills. The cops are so well oiled that they leave him alone. Poison won't let a word in his papers. The other rags follow his lead. Everyone is making money, as far as I can see, except the girls themselves."

"Any girls missing?"

Henry nodded. "The Missing People's Bureau has been taken over by a guy named Goldburg. He's in Grantham's pocket. No one does anything about the girls. They just write up particulars and that's all. The increase in missing girls is up forty per cent. They're gettin' girls in from outside too. The guys I've met who've been to the houses tell me that every week there's a new set of girls. They're drilled in every form of vice imaginable."

Jay rubbed his hands. "I'm goin' after this racket, Chief," he said. "I'll smash it or bust."

Henry looked worried. "It's too big for you," he said. "These guys are makin' dough now. They're dangerous."

"If I can find out anythin' to prove it I'll turn the whole thing over to the F.B.I.," Jay said. "I ain't tacklin' them single-handed."

"What the hell do you think the F.B.I. are doin' now?" Henry snapped. "They're just waitin' to pounce. This guy is so smart they can't move yet. If they catch him in the Mann Act they can move. But no one knows how he gets his girls across the State line."

Jay got up. "Well, I'm free. I've got nothin' to do. So I may as well look this over. If I can tie Poison up to this I'll do it."

Henry reached out his hand. "Good luck," he said. "If I'd the guts I'd get out of this game myself. I'm too old now to look for anything else."

Jay shook hands with him. "Leave it to me," he said. "If I want any help I'll come and see you."

Henry smiled crookedly. "After today, Jay," he said, "you and I've got to take different roads. Poison will make me go after you."

Jay went to the door. "Okay," he said, "I'll remember that," and he went out fast.

6

September 7th, 10.45 p.m.

The smart little dance-hall was crowded. Soft lights, heady swing, and laughter. It drew the girls and their partners like moths to a naked flame.

A tall, good-looking Jew, well dressed, a small diamond glittering in his tie, glanced carefully round the room as he sat at a quiet table. Particularly, his eyes dwelt on the line of unattended girls who sat chattering to each other, laughing and giggling, but hoping for a male to take them on to the floor.

The Jew examined each girl swiftly as his eye swept down the line. He selected one. She was pretty, young, with a nice figure. She looked a lot more lively than the others, and in a mild way was trying to catch the eyes of the guys who every now and then walked along to find a new partner.

The Jew knew that this particular dance-hall always had a lot more girls than partners. It was a happy-hunting-ground for him. He got languidly to his feet and walked over to the line. He made straight for the girl he had selected.

He said in a soft voice, "I'd like a dance if you'll give me one."

She got up at once. "Sure," she said. She knew he was a Jew, but he was tall and handsome. She didn't mind.

They danced in silence. He knew his stuff and she thought

he was a swell dancer. When the band cut out he took her back to her seat. He was satisfied she was the right type.

"That was grand," he said. "I'd like another later."

He went out almost immediately and signalled to a car, parked across the road. Then he went back to the hall. The band had started playing again, and he saw she was dancing with a little guy who kept tripping over her feet.

He sat down at the table. He was used to waiting. At last the dance finished and she went back to her seat.

When the short interval was over he got up and went across to her quickly. She saw him coming and got up with a smile. That was what he wanted. She was already getting used to him.

As he swung her through the crowd he hummed the melody the band was playing. He could sing.

She said, "Nice voice."

"Nice girl," he returned, smiling.

She laughed a little. "You don't mean that, do you?"

"Sure. You're so nice I can't believe you're here on your own."

She pouted a little. "I haven't got a regular boy."

"Then I'm lucky," he said.

"Don't be smart."

"When this dance's over, will you have somethin' to drink?"

She shook her head. "I don't."

"Well, come and watch me."

She didn't say anything, and the Jew grinned to himself. He was pretty experienced. This was going to be a push-over.

The band ceased abruptly, and he led her back to his table. They sat down together.

"I bet your Pa doesn't know you're out," he said, offering her a cigarette.

She giggled. "How did you know? Pa hates me dancing. I sneak out once a week. Even Ma thinks I'm in bed."

The Jew smiled. "You're a bad girl. I ought to take you home."

They both laughed. A waiter came and hovered near them. "Come on, have a beer," the Jew said. "It's from the ice here, and it's swell."

She said, "Just one, then, but I don't usually drink with strangers."

The Jew gave the order to the waiter. "You're quite right," he said. "A nice-lookin' girl like you can't be too careful." He put his fingers into his vest pocket and took out a little white pill. He kept the pill between his first and second fingers. The girl didn't notice anything.

When the waiter brought the drinks the Jew pointed suddenly behind the girl. "Who's that guy?" he asked.

His hand hovered over her glass as she turned her head, and the pill slid into the liquid.

She shook her head. "I don't know. Why?"

"I've seen him about a lot. Wondered who he was. Quite a guy, ain't he?"

She turned back to the beer. It looked very inviting. He raised his glass. "Hey, beautiful," he said with a flourish.

They both drank deeply. She shuddered when she put the glass down. "It's horrid stuff," she said.

He laughed. "Beer's an acquired taste, baby; you'll grow to love it." He pushed back his chair. "Come on, let's dance."

Halfway across the room she lost time. He changed step and steered her towards the exit. She suddenly grew very heavy and her hands clutched at his arms.

"I'm goin' to faint," she said in a far-away voice. "Get me out of here."

He was already leading her to the door. One of his arms was round her waist and he had to support her. No one noticed anything wrong. When they got out into the open she collapsed and sank down on her knees.

The closed car swung across the road and one of the doors opened.

The Jew picked her up and shoved her hastily into the car. The door slammed and the car drove away very fast.

The Jew watched the tail-light disappear and then he went back to the dance-hall. It was easy. He sat down at the table again and took out a little note-book. He made an entry. Then he put the note-book away and sat back, his eyes once more searching the line of girls waiting for partners.

7

September 8th, 9 a.m.

Raven opened his eyes. He had a knack of being instantly awake after a heavy sleep. He never struggled back into consciousness. One moment he was asleep, then next he was fully awake. He stared up at the ornate ceiling, feeling the soft comfort of the bed under him.

Three months ago he had been a bum. Now he was powerful, rich and feared, but he was smart enough to know it couldn't last. Some time someone would squeal, and he'd have to go into hiding. It would be different now. He had money banked in several banks under different names. He had a lot of money in the apartment. He could skip to Europe if necessary. That sent his thoughts in another direction. Why not skip out while the going was good? Grantham could run this racket now he'd got it started. He could go to France or to the Argentine. There was a lot of scope there for a guy with his brains.

He turned and looked at Sadie, who was sleeping by his side. He was pleased with her. She'd got class, she was a looker, and she didn't make trouble. He'd tamed her all right.

He leant upon his elbow and studied her thoughtfully. She had little dark smudges under her eyes and her mouth was a little slack. Still, she was a looker for all that. She'd last for another couple of months, then he'd send her back to one of his houses and find someone else. His hand groped for the bell, and he rang it. Then he climbed out of the bed and went into the bathroom. By the time he'd shaved breakfast had been brought in.

Sadie woke up. She yawned and stretched her long white arms. Raven poured himself out a cup of coffee. "Do you want some?" he said.

"Might as well," she said listlessly, climbing out of bed. She struggled into a wrap and went off to the bathroom.

Raven glanced through the paper and then chucked it on one side. He found a pile of letters on the tray and began to glance through them. Most of them were for bills. They were all addressed to J. J. Cruise, the name he had adopted when he moved into the St. Louis Hotel. The last envelope was bulky and it contained a catalogue of trains. He was reading this carefully when Sadie came back.

She poured out some coffee and sat watching him indifferently. A great change had taken place since she had gone away with O'Hara. She knew it herself. She could no longer struggle against this man. He had proved himself so utterly ruthless and hateful that her resistance had been completely shattered. She no longer lived. She sat about waiting to obey his commands. Her terror for him had long burnt itself out. It was just a matter of automatically complying with his wishes. She found that if she did what she was told he was bearable. They went out together, lived together and slept together. She had no animation, but he seemed satisfied with being seen about with her. She didn't care what people thought or who saw her. Her will had ceased to exist.

The catalogue revived his interest in the trains. He looked up. "Get that train outfit," he said. "Put it up in the other room. I'll amuse myself with it, I think."

She put down her cup and went out of the room immediately. Raven scowled and stared after her. Sometimes her obedience bored him. He wished she'd refuse so that he could vent his spite on her. He shrugged and, still frowning, continued to turn the pages of the catalogue.

The house phone buzzed and he shouted for her to answer it. She came out of the other room and, after listening at the receiver, said, "A Mr. Grantham wants to see you."

Raven nodded. "Send him up," he said.

She spoke again to the clerk and then went back into the other room. Raven could hear her setting out the tracks.

A knock sounded on the door and Grantham walked in.

Raven nodded. "Come on in," he said. "Nice little place this, hey?"

Grantham hadn't been up before. He glanced around. "Very," he said shortly, taking off his light dust-coat. He selected a chair and sat down.

Raven watched him narrowly. "Well, what's wrong?"

Grantham came to the point at once. "Ellinger's in town," he said.

Raven shook his head. "I don't know him."

"Ellinger is a reporter on the *St. Louis Banner*. He covers the crime angle. We've had trouble with him before. Now it looks as if he means to stick his neck out. He's left the Banner and has been makin' a lot of enquiries about me. I don't like it."

Raven sneered. "You guys are helpless," he said. "Scare him. Turn some of the boys on to him. He'll quit."

"He's not that type of guy," he said. "The harder we try an' scare him, the harder he'll stick."

"Then arrange a little accident. Don't bother me with these trifles." Raven finished his coffee. "How's the business goin'?"

Grantham nodded. "It's goin' all right." He sounded doubtful.

"Well, what is it? Ain't you satisfied?"

"Of course I am, but don't you think we're takin' a hell of a risk? Some of these girls will squeal. They're bound to. I think we ought to stick to the professional. Seventy-five per cent of the girls you send me are kidnapped into the game. It's getting tough keeping them in order. There's a big yap coming from Denver and Cleveland about the number of girls that are missing."

Raven laughed. "You're just a small-time hick," he said. "Guys don't want the professional type of hustler. They want fresh innocent stuff, and you know it. The guys that pay big dough don't give a damn where they come from or what song they sing as long as they have them. So you can't keep them in order. I've got a little jane who was traded. I'll show you how I've made her toe the line."

He called, "Come here."

Sadie came in. "Yes?" she said.

Grantham stared at her and then went pale. He recognized her at once. He'd been wondering where the hell she had got to. Carrie had been sent to Kansas City, and he had lost track of her. He had made efforts to trace her as he knew Sadie would be with her, and he'd failed.

Sadie looked at him, recognized him as the man who got her into this trouble, and flinched away from him. Raven noticed the changes in their expressions.

He said to her roughly, "Get out!" And when she had gone he turned on Grantham. "You know her?"

Grantham wondered if this was a trap. He eased his collar

with a limp finger. "Yeah," he said, "she was one of the first girls I shanghaied."

Raven nodded. "That's right," he said; "I found her at the nigger's house. She's got reason to hate you, hasn't she?" and he laughed.

Grantham was very uneasy. He wasn't sure how much Raven knew. If Raven had an inkling that Sadie could name him as Mendetta's killer, surely he wouldn't have her around? He was so bewildered that he wanted to get away and think about it. He moved to the door. "So you think Ellinger can be taken care of?" he said.

Raven studied his nails. "Why not?" he said, pulling his dressing-gown cord tighter round his waist. "Make an accident of it... you know."

Grantham nodded. "I'll get it done," he said, and went away.

Raven sat brooding. There was something he couldn't understand about Sadie. First Carrie and now Grantham. They both showed uneasiness when they were in his presence and Sadie's. He went into the other room.

Sadie was kneeling amid the tracks and the big outfit. She looked up quickly.

"Old pal of yours, huh?" Raven said.

She looked at him searchingly and then went on adjusting the line.

Raven felt a sudden vicious spurt of rage run through him as he stood behind her. He knelt down at her side and pushed her over. She fell off balance across the tracks and her shoulders flattened a miniature station. She gave a little cry as the tin of the station dug into her flesh.

Grinning at her, Raven pushed her flat and then, amid the railway, flattened by their bodies, he had her.

8

September 8th, 10.30 a.m.

Jay Ellinger parked his car in the big courtyard of the Preston Building and asked the commissionaire for Benny Perminger.

The commissionaire shook his head. "He left here a couple of weeks ago," he said. "Mr. Caston would tell you where he went."

Jay followed him into the reception hall. After a delay of phoning the commissionaire jerked his head to the elevator. "Third floor. Sixth door on the right," he said.

Jay found Caston looking worried. He shook hands with him and accepted a chair.

"You a friend of Perminger's?" Caston asked.

Jay nodded. "I've been out of town for some time," he explained. "I wanted to get in touch with him. It's important."

Caston played with his penholder. "Well, I'm glad someone wants to find him," he said. "I've been worried about that guy."

"He's left here?"

Caston pulled a face. "Between you an' me, he was hoofed out. I liked that guy, you know. He was a good salesman. Then his wife ran away from him. That put him on the skids. I've never seen a man go to pieces so quickly."

"What happened then?"

"He began hittin' the bottle. It got so bad that we couldn't keep him any longer. We all tried to hide it up, but the management got on to it in the end. He didn't get any business. We had complaints. It was a bad show."

Jay grunted. "Well, where is he? What's he doin' now?"

Caston shook his head. "I don't know," he said. "The last time I heard from him he was working for an addressing agency. Not much in that, you know." He opened one of his desk drawers and searched, then he produced a little note-book. "He's staying at an apartment house on 26th Street. If you can do anything for that guy I'll be mighty pleased. He wants looking after."

Jay scribbled the address down and got up. "Thanks, Mr. Caston," he said, "I'll go an' see him."

The apartment house reminded Jay of Fletcher. He thought, as he went up the steps, that this Slave racket was not only ruining the lives of hundreds of girls, but its repercussions were affecting the lives of their menfolk. It made him all the more determined to burst it open.

On the top floor he found Benny seated at a table scribbling away at a furious pace. A large stack of addressed envelopes lay on the table and bundles of other envelopes lay around the room. Benny looked a complete wreck. He hadn't shaved for several days, and his eyes were heavy and glazed. A strong smell of stale whisky came from him as he lurched to his feet, nearly overturning the table.

He said, "For God's sake," and shook hands eagerly. "I've given you up. Sit down, buddy, an' have a drink."

Jay looked round the grimy room. One glance was enough to tell him that Perminger was up against it. He refused the drink, but lit a cigarette. Benny poured himself a long shot of neat spirit. He held the unlabelled bottle to the light and scowled. "Hell! Someone's been stealing this stuff." He said angrily, "There was half a bottle here last night."

Jay said, "Forget it. I want to talk to you. What's all this business?" He waved his hand around the room.

Benny shrugged. "I gotta live," he said. "It's a lousy job, but it pays for this." He tapped the bottle and winked.

Jay got up and wandered to the window. "You didn't turn up anything when I was away?" he said over his shoulder.

"Listen, I ain't interested any more." Benny's voice was sullen.

"Lost your guts?" Jay said.

"Yeah, so would you."

"Well, come on, let's have it. Have you found out anything about your wife?"

Benny poured himself out another drink. "I haven't got a wife," he said.

Jay lost patience with him. He came back to the table. "Listen. Don't be a heel. Your wife disappeared, didn't she? She's probably working for this Slave racket right now. I'm going to find her, and you're going to help me."

Benny's face was white and his eyes looked wild. "No, you're not," he said, speaking through clenched teeth. "She wasn't slaved. I've seen her. It was a trick. She's livin' with some guy at the St. Louis Hotel. I even spoke to her, but she cut me dead. Wouldn't even look at me."

Jay stiffened to attention. "You're sure of this?" he demanded.

"Think I'd make a thing like that up?" Benny said, looking at him with hurt, angry eyes. "Of course I'm sure. She's livin' with that guy in luxury. That's what she's always wanted. She was always bellyachin' about doin' the washin' and lookin' after the apartment. Now she's got what she wants. The dirty little chippy."

"You may be misjudging her, Perminger," Jay reminded him. "She might have to be there."

Benny sneered. "Don't talk bull. I tell you I spoke to her. She just looked through me. She could have got away if she wanted to. She was by herself. I followed her to the hotel. I found out from the porter all about them. The guy's name's Cruise. She's posin' as his wife."

Jay sat down limply. He felt the ground had been cut from under him. "Who is this guy Cruise?" he asked.

Benny shrugged. "I don't know, an' I don't care. I ain't goin' to start anythin' with him. If that's the life she likes, she can have it. I'm through with her."

Jay got slowly to his feet. He felt that it was only wasting time. He said, "Well, I'm sorry, Perminger. It's tough," and shook hands.

Out in the street he paused before getting into his car. On the face of it it looked as if the whole of the business had fallen to pieces. The only thing he had to go on was Fletcher's testimony, and Fletcher was dead. He got in the car and engaged the gears.

Who was this Cruise? Had he anything to do with Grantham? Could it be possible that Perminger's wife had really gone off with him and had made up the note about going to police headquarters? It didn't seem likely. There was something wrong there. He made up his mind abruptly to take a look at Cruise. If he looked all right, then he'd try some other angle, but if he didn't, then he'd keep a watch on him.

He drove over to the St. Louis Hotel and parked. He knew the house dick and went straight to his little office.

The house dick was resting his feet and reading the newspaper. He glanced up as Jay came in.

"Hyah, Harris," Jay said, shaking hands. "How you makin' out?"

Harris was a little plump guy, who lived in a bowler hat. He shook hands suspiciously. "Well, what is it this time?" he said. "I haven't been bothered by you for months."

Jay grinned at him. "I've been covering the Tammany Hall trial. Too bad that guy got off."

Harris grunted. "They'll get him the next time, you see," he said. "Now what do you want? I'm busy."

"All right, all right, keep your shirt on." Jay grinned at him. "Can you give me a line on a guy named Cruise who hangs out here?"

Harris's little eyes opened. "Aaah!" he said. "Now, I was wonderin' when you boys were goin' to get on to him. What makes you ask?"

Jay shrugged. "Curiosity. I've never seen the guy, but I've heard about him."

Harris wasn't to be drawn. "What have you heard?" he asked, looking cunning.

Jay knew there was only one short cut to getting anything out of Harris. Reluctantly he took out his roll and thumbed off ten bucks. He dangled the notes in front of Harris's nose. "No questions," he said.

Harris grinned and grabbed the notes. He tucked them in his vest pocket. "Well," he said, "I don't like him. I don't like the mob he has up in his suite. I don't like the dame who lives with him."

Jay waited patiently.

"For one thing," Harris went on, "no respectable guy associates with the kind of hoods that go up there. I've had my eye on him ever since he moved in. He's a mean-lookin' guy himself. I'll swear the dame ain't his wife. She acts sortta strange. She's scared of him. Three punks see him every day. They drive up in the staff elevator. You ought to see the way one of them dresses. Still, they pay all right and we've got nothing against them, but I'm watching 'em."

This sounded promising to Jay. He said, "Can I get a room on their floor, Harris?"

"Like that, is it?" Harris looked interested. "Yeah, I guess that could be arranged. Shall I fix it?"

Jay nodded. "Another thing. Maybe this guy's got a record. Suppose you get his prints?"

Harris sneered. "Talk sense. I can't do a thing like that."

Jay took out his silver cigarette-case. "Take this up to him. Push it into his hands. Tell him you found it outside his apartment and you think it's his. Then bring it back and let me have it. I'll take it to the F.B.I. for a test."

Harris gaped at him. "Jeeze," he exclaimed, "that's smart!"

He took the case from Jay and got up. "I'll see him right away. You wait here."

He came back again after some time, his fat face beaming. "That's a laugh," he declared. "You've lost your case. He took it all right, said it was his, gave me a buck for my trouble and shut the door in my face."

Jay sat back limply. "Goddam it," he said with a weak grin, "that shows he's a crook."

Harris nodded. "I've fixed a room for you," he said, "you can move up whenever you like."

Jay got to his feet. "I'm on my way," he said, and left Harris still grinning.

9

September 8th, 4.30 p.m.

Lu Eller walked casually down the corridor leading to Raven's suite. He knew Raven was out. He had seen him leave not five minutes ago. He'd been waiting for him to go for a long time. Even now he'd got to be careful. Someone else beside Sadie might be in the suite.

He listened outside the door for several minutes, but couldn't hear anything. Then he knocked softly.

Sadie came to the door. When she saw him she started back, trying to close the door, but Lu'd got his foot in the way. "Raven in?" he asked pleasantly, tipping his hat.

She shook her head. "No—go away. No one's in."

That's what Lu wanted to hear. He smiled. "He said I was to wait. He won't be long."

Sadie was terrified of him. "You can't come in," she said; "wait downstairs."

Lu had heard tales about Raven and Sadie. "He said I was to wait here," he told her firmly. "You don't want him to get mad with you?"

She dropped her hand from the door and stepped back. Lu

looked hastily up and down the corridor and then came in. He shut the door.

Sadie backed away from him, and then almost ran into her bedroom.

Grantham had been very plain. "She's got to go, Lu," he had said. "We can't use her against Raven any more. He's doin' well, an' any time she might spill it. Raven would rumble it at once. No, she's got to go."

Lu eased his fingers a little. He'd got to work fast. Raven might change his mind and come back any moment. Lu was a little nervous. She wasn't small and she might be stronger than he could manage. There was no question of shooting. His hand groped round to his hip pocket and he drew a short heavy-bladed knife from its sheath. He slipped the blade up his cuff, holding the handle hidden in his palm.

He went over to the bedroom door and rapped.

She said with a little catch in her voice, "What do you want?"

Softly he turned the handle and looked in. "Can you fix me a drink, lady?"

"Get out of here!" Sadie was frightened of him.

"Aw, come on, lady, Raven said for you to make me at home." Lu smiled at her. He edged his way further into the room.

"Get out, or I'll scream," Sadie said, retreating to the other side of the room.

"What's bitin' you, lady?" Lu asked, moving forward very slowly. "I just want a drink. Ain't anythin' in that."

He was halfway across the room by now. Sadie saw the cold, merciless gleam in his eyes and she screamed. Lu swore softly and jumped forward. The blade gleamed as it swung towards her. She dodged desperately, thudded against the wall and fell.

Lu grunted and stabbed down at her. She rolled away, the knife cutting through her sleeve and making a long scratch on her arm. She screamed again.

Lunging again, Lu nearly had her this time, but with unsuspected speed she again dodged him, and ran past him into the outer room.

Lu was getting into a panic. She'd have all the hotel up in

a minute. He went after her. She was just opening the front door to get into the corridor. He didn't hesitate. His arm flashed up and the knife hissed through the air. Sadie heard the sound and flung herself sideways. The knife buried itself in the fleshy part of her arm. She fell on her knees with a faint cry of pain.

As Lu ran towards her a thunder-bolt struck him. Jay, hearing the uproar, had come to investigate. He saw Sadie lying on the floor and Lu coming at her, his face livid with fury and panic, and Jay launched himself full tilt at him.

The two men went down in a heap. Lu brought his knees up and tossed Jay away. Both of them scrambled to their feet. Lu's hand flew to his gun, but Jay was already on him again and they went down in a mass of flaying arms and legs. Jay brought over his right and hit Lu hard on his cheek-bone. Lu's hands got a grip on Jay's throat and they rolled over and over across the corridor.

Jay got hold of Lu's wrists and tried to break his hold, but Lu was too strong for him. Already the pressure on his windpipe was beginning to tell. His head seemed to be expanding like an inflated toy balloon. He drove his fist into Lu's face. The grip loosened as Lu grunted with the unexpected pain. Jay hit him again and wriggled clear. Lu recognized him then. In that split second of recognition Lu realized that this guy must not escape. Grantham had given instructions to shoot at sight. Now he was here, right in the middle of everything.

He groped for his gun, swearing because it had caught in the lining of his pocket. He jerked feverishly on the handle.

Jay came at him again, his fists hit Lu on the side of his head and face, smashing him to the floor. The gun came away from his pocket.

"No, you don't," Jay panted, stamping on Lu's wrist. The gun dropped on the thick carpet, and Jay kicked it away.

Lu dived after the gun, stooped to grab it, and got a paralysing kick that sent him hurtling down the corridor. He picked himself up and ran. Jay chased him to the end of the corridor, but Lu beat him to it. He fell down the first flight of stairs, and then, picking himself up, he beat it as if hell were at his heels.

Jay dusted himself down and went back to Sadie, who was half sitting up watching with fascinated eyes the steady flow of blood from her arm.

Jay picked her up. "Take it easy, sister," he said, "I'll get you out of here."

He carried her into his room and kicked the door closed. When he put her on the bed he ran back and turned the key in the lock. Then he went into the bathroom, grabbed a couple of small hand-towels, and stopped the bleeding.

She went very white when he took the knife out, but she didn't faint.

He said, "That's fine. I'll get you a drink. Just lie quiet."

He rang down to Harris. "Listen, bud, I've had a little trouble on up my floor," he said, when Harris came on to the line. "Will you come on up and keep an eye on me?"

Harris said, "What sort of trouble?"

"Now don't start askin' questions, come up an' bring a rod." He hung up with a grim little smile.

He fixed Sadie a drink from the small flask he always carried around with him, and then went out into the corridor to meet Harris.

Harris came up at a rim. His big face was alight with excitement. "What is it?" he asked.

"If this guy Cruise shows up I want you to tell him that some hood tried to stab his wife. Tell him the cops took both of them down to the station. For God's sake don't let him know I've got her in this room."

"I can't do that," Harris exploded; "it'll cost me my job."

"Do it," Jay said shortly; "this guy won't go near the cops, I'm sure of that. If he gets an idea that I've got her here he's goin' to get very tough. If you do this I'll give you twenty bucks."

Harris's eyes brightened. "Let's have it," he said quickly.

Jay gave him the money. "Look, go into his apartment and get that cigarette-case of mine. Snap into it."

Harris returned in a few minutes, holding the case. "Here it is. Now what?"

"Just hang around the corridor until he comes back. You'd better make a good show or else that guy will do things to you." Jay left him and went back to Sadie. She was lying on the bed. Although she was still very white, she looked stronger.

Jay locked the door and came over to her. "I'm Jay Ellinger, late of the *St. Louis Banner*," he said. "You're Mrs. Perminger, ain't you?"

Sadie sat up, once more terrified. "No—no! You've made a mistake. I'm Mrs. Cruise," she said.

Jay sat down on the bed. He took out a packet of cigarettes and offered her one. "Go on," he said, when she refused. "It'll steady you."

She took it nervously, looking at him all the time. Sitting close to her, he could see the ravishes of time and horror stamped on her face. He could see the hard lines, the frightened eyes, and he knew that she'd been through some terrible experiences.

When he had lighted the cigarettes he said, "This is your chance to get out of this mess. I know you're Mrs. Perminger. I was talkin' to your husband a while ago."

Sadie looked at him, and then her face crumpled. She hastily put up her hands and began to cry.

Jay said, "Take it easy. You're safe now. Tell me. It's true, isn't it?"

She nodded without speaking.

"Now listen, Mrs. Perminger. It's goin' to be all right. You've got to take me into your confidence. I can guess something of what happened to you but I want the full story. You saw the guy who killed Mendetta, didn't you?"

She sat up, terrified. "Who told you?" she gasped.

"I guessed that's how they tricked you to leave your apartment, wasn't it? That would explain the note you left."

Sadie nodded. "I saw him coming out of the room. Then a policeman came and made me go away with that man you were fighting with. They took me to a house and kept me there. There was a negress who beat me. I tried and tried to stick it out, but I couldn't. She beat me every hour of the day. I had to give in." She sat up and beat her knees with her fists. Her face was twisted with fear and rage. "Do you understand? I wouldn't do what she wanted me to do. So she kept on and on and on. Every day they tied me to the bed. There was a nigger who stripped me... Do you understand that? She let him put his filthy hands on me. He stood and laughed at me when she beat me. I tried... but I couldn't stand it any more." She sobbed again. "What was I to do? There are other girls, decent girls like me. They were brought to the house and men were sent into their rooms. I can still hear their screams. Beasts of men used to pay money—lots of money—to assault them. They liked them to fight and scream—they paid more and more money if they really fought. It was horrible."

Jay tapped off the ash from his cigarette. This made him feel bad.

"Then this man Cruise came one day. He inspected all the girls. He took them all away. I don't know what happened to them. He treated them as if they were cattle. He took me. He brought me here. I was to be his slave. Well, I was crazy. I refused. I told him to get out. So what do you think he did?" Her sobbing was so violent he could hardly hear what she was saying. "He tied me to the bed and he—he poured turpentine over me. Do you know what that means? He left me lying there all night. I was gagged. I couldn't move, and it burnt.... Oh. God! How it burnt!"

Jay thought: "Here it is. Right with the lid off. This is the stuff that I want. I can start somethin' now." He said to her, "Grantham? Does he come into this?"

She nodded miserably. "He works for Cruise," she gasped. "He comes here and they talk. I've heard things. They got houses all over the town. They get girls from Denver, from Springfields—everywhere. Don't you understand? They're good girls. They take them from their homes and they make them do this work. Oh, you must stop it! You must stop it!"

Jay patted her hand. "I'll stop it," he said grimly. He got up and reached for the phone. "Give me the Federal Bureau of Investigation," he said.

10

September 8th, 5 p.m.

Grantham looked round the large room, his face cold and sneering. There were some thirty girls standing around the room. Some of them had on wraps, others just wore knickers and black stockings. They were all looking sullen and were only suppressing their fury because Madam, a big, hard-featured woman, stood behind Grantham.

Grantham said, "You girls've got to shake up your ideas. We've done badly here this week. I'm going to try a little experiment. Next week you'll all go on a commission basis. See how you get on with that." There was a low murmur from the girls. Madam said, "Shut up, you!"

Grantham's lips twisted into a sneering smile. He turned to Madam. "You've been too soft with these bitches," he said. "Get hold of the ringleaders and turn them over to my men. They'll knock the starch out of them. What the hell do they think they're here for—fun?"

Out of the crowd of girls Fan suddenly pressed forward. "Hey, bastard," she said, "let me tell you something. Since you've taken over, we girls ain't had any breaks. We don't get money. We don't know how much we've earned. Now you say you're just giving us commission."

Grantham looked her over. "Who do you think you're talkin' to?" he said.

"Heel number one," Fan returned. "I for one ain't goin' to take any more from you—see?"

Grantham turned to Madam. "What you waitin' for? That's one of 'em who wants handlin'."

Madam walked over to Fan, who stood her ground, her eyes flashing dangerously. She said, "Lay off, or you'll get hurt."

There was a long pause, then the door jerked open and Lu came in with a rush. His face was covered with livid bruises and his collar and tie were missing.

Grantham stared at him. "What the hell—?"

"Come on, boss," Lu panted, "I've got a car outside. The lid's blown off. Let's go."

"You mad?" Grantham said, forgetting that the girls were listening curiously.

"I tell you we've got to beat it. That swine Ellinger's got the Perminger dame. She'll spill everything."

Grantham went white with rage. "I told you to get her," he snarled.

"I know—I know. Don't stand arguing. I tried. He got there first. Come on, boss."

Grantham turned to the door. Fan got in his way and he shoved her to one side. "Get out of my way, you cow!" he shouted.

Fan seemed to go mad. She sprang at him, shrieking for the other girls to join in. Grantham flung her away, and then went down under a heap of furious harpies.

Lu hesitated, then turned and bolted for the door. Julie threw herself in his way and they went down on the floor together. Three other girls piled on top of him.

Fan was shrieking like a madwoman. "Give it to the swines! Tear 'em apart!" she yelled, making a dive at Madam, who ran screaming out of the room.

Grantham fought his way to his feet, hitting out right and left with his fists. He was badly frightened. It was only by swinging his arms violently that he kept off the claw-like fingers that quested for his face. He took a couple of steps back as the shrieking girls bore down on him, and then his heel was seized by one of the fallen ones and he went over with a thud that shook the room.

Lu was bawling for help as he twisted and squirmed under the mass of girls. Grantham had his hands too full to do anything. He beat them off a second time and got to the door.

"Don't let him get out!" Fan screamed. "Bring the bastard down!" She rushed across the room and flung herself on Grantham, biting and tearing at him with her teeth and nails.

Grantham swung his fist and hit her in her throat, sending her reeling backwards. He pulled open the door and got out into the hall.

Andree and Julie pulled him down as he reached the front door. Andree traced three livid marks on his face with her nails. Grantham began to sob for breath. He kicked them away and bolted upstairs.

Lu was helpless in the hands of the girls who had seized him. There was a girl hanging on to each of his limbs, pinning him to the floor. His clothes were in ribbons and his face was a mask of blood where they had clawed him. He screamed on a high note with terror as they dragged the rest of his clothes off him.

Fan fought her way to him, pulling off the girls and throwing them on one side. "Let me get at the heel!" she shrilled. "I'll teach him somethin'. Get out of the way!"

The girls drew back, their faces savage and lustful. They crowded round again, as Fan knelt over the sobbing man.

"Get a knife, someone," she shouted. "I'm goin' to fix this guy so he doesn't play around any more."

A knife materialized from somewhere and was handed over the heads of the girls. Fan seized it.

Lu gave a horrible strangled scream when he saw the flash of steel, and when she laid hands on him he nearly went mad. "Don't do it—don't do it!" he screamed. "No—no—no—aaah! Aaaaah!"

The girls suddenly drew away, leaving him lying there. A long ribbon of blood ran towards them so that they drew further back, shuddering.

Fan, her eyes gleaming madly, shrilled, "What are you waitin' for? Where's the other one?"

In a body they stampeded for the door. Andree and Julie had already gone upstairs. They could hear them thumping on a door.

Fan, her hands covered in blood, ran up the stairs, with the others behind her. They brushed the two girls away from the door and threw themselves forward. The door creaked and bulged, but held.

Grantham backed against the wall, terrified. He rushed to the window and threw it up. Far below him he could see cars passing and people moving about in the streets. He leant far out of the window and began to yell at the top of his voice.

Faces turned towards him. People stopped and pointed. Cars came to a standstill, and people got out to look at him. He saw a policeman move towards the house with a slow measured tread. Behind him he heard the door creak, and he yelled again, his voice going off pitch with terror.

Then with a crash the door flew open, and he spun round, his back to the window.

Fan stood there, her hair wild and her eyes savage. He saw the bloodstained knife gripped in her hand and he turned back to the window. He heard his own voice screaming in panic as he tried to climb out.

They all came across the room in a wave. Hands seized him and dragged him back. He went down under them with a thin wail of terror.

11

September 8th, 5.30 p.m.

Raven glanced at the clock and stood up. It was time he got back to his hotel. He nodded to Maltz. "It's goin' all right," he said. "We'll have to open some more houses. The girls are comin' in now faster than we can handle them."

Maltz grunted. "The cops at Denver are workin' on this, boss," he said. "There's been a hell of a lot of squawks from that town. Maybe we ought to ease up on the girls there." Raven nodded. "Sure," he said; "put a little more pressure on Cleveland. When things start getting hot, try somewhere else."

He went to the door. "I'm goin' back now," he said. "You might go over to the 22nd tonight. I'm expecting a batch of girls to come in. Grantham's gettin' too busy to handle that sort of thing now."

Maltz said he would, and Raven went out. He walked down the stairs, his face thoughtful. All the afternoon he had been worrying. He knew someone wanted to get his finger-prints. When the St. Louis house dick had brought him the cigarette-case his suspicions had been aroused. It couldn't be the authorities. They would never have used a broken-down flatfoot like Harris.

The last three months of easy living had not blunted his finely developed sense of self-preservation. He had got on too well to risk anything now.

Out in the street he hesitated before calling a taxi. Something told him that he shouldn't return to the hotel. Yet, he told himself savagely, he'd got to. All his dough was there.

As he neared the hotel he leant forward and told the driver to go straight on past. He crouched back in the cab and examined the hotel carefully as they went by. He saw nothing there to alarm him. Still he wasn't satisfied. He stopped the taxi at the next block and paid him off. Then he went into a phone booth and rang his apartment. The clerk said apologetically that he could get no answer. He asked sharply if his wife was out. The clerk told him he hadn't seen her go. Raven hung up.

By now he was a little alarmed. He wondered if Grantham

knew anything. When he rang Grantham's office he was told that he was out, but was expected any minute.

"Where's he gone?" he asked.

The girl said, "To Madam Lacey's house."

Raven hung up and immediately rang Madam Lacey's. A hard voice answered him. It was a man's voice he couldn't place. He asked for Grantham.

"Who are you?" the voice snapped.

Raven sensed that it was a cop. He felt cold sweat suddenly break out under his arms. "Tell him it's Fleming," he said; "I want to talk to him."

"He's busy right now," the voice said. "Suppose you come down."

"I'll be right along," Raven said, and hung up. There was something wrong. He rang up Maltz.

"Go over to the hotel and sniff around," he said, after explaining what had happened. "Don't give yourself away. Just poke around quietly and meet me at Franky's in an hour's time."

Maltz said he would.

Raven came out of the phone-box and lit a cigarette. He hailed a taxi and gave Madam Lacey's address. "I want you to cruise past the joint slowly, but you're not to stop."

The taxi-driver said he'd do that and set the cab rolling. They reached the house in a few minutes, and Raven could see something was wrong. There were two police cars and an ambulance standing outside. A policeman stood at the door frowning at the large collection of people standing staring.

At the end of the road Raven paid off the taxi and walked slowly back towards the house. He kept on the opposite side of the road, his hand touching the handle of his hidden gun. He mingled with the crowd and stood watching.

Three patrol wagons came racing down the street, their sirens wailing, and drew up outside the house. The crowd surged forward, carrying Raven with them.

"What the hell's going on here?" he asked a guy who stood near him.

"They're raidin' a brothel," the guy said with evident relish. "Seems a riot broke out inside. They say the dames in there set about two fellas and killed them."

Raven started. "What do you mean—killed them?"

"That's right," a sheep-faced man broke in. "Two punks who ran the house. The girls got tough an' gave them the works—serve the lousy punks right."

Just then the front door opened and the police began to bundle the girls out into the street. The crowd raised an ironic cheer. The girls were herded into the wagons, cops applying their night-sticks to their backsides as they fought and protested. It was a real outing for the crowd. The sheep-faced man yelled, "I bet those cops'll have a treat tonight." The crowd raised a loud laugh. "Can we help you, copper," another man bawled, "or can you manage that little lot yourself?"

Raven recognized Fan, Julie and Andree. He noticed they were handcuffed. Fan was being very troublesome, and the cops were treating her rough.

Raven was livid with suppressed rage. Each one of those girls brought him in a large income. What the hell did the cops mean by breaking into one of his houses? Then he remembered what the sheep-faced man had said. Uneasily, he waited. The wagons moved off, and then two white-coated attendants came out, carrying a stretcher. The crowd gave a groan of satisfaction and shoved forward some more. By stretching his neck Raven caught a glimpse of a figure covered with a white sheet being slid into the ambulance. Almost immediately two more attendants came out carrying another stretcher.

"What did I tell you?" the sheep-faced man demanded triumphantly. "Killed two guys those girls did. An' serve 'em right, I say."

Raven had seen quite enough. It was dangerous to stay here any longer. He broke away from the crowd and walked hurriedly away. His brain was on fire with worry. Maybe Maltz would find out something. It was obviously very unsafe to return to his hotel. He passed a telephone booth, hesitated, and then went in. He rang up the D.A.'s office.

"Hackensfield?" he asked, when a man answered the phone. "This is a friend of Grantham. What's happened? What the hell are you raiding one of our houses' for?"

"Who are you? What's your name?" Hackensfield demanded. He sounded tough.

"Never mind who I am. If you want to stay on our payroll you'd better get those girls off at once," Raven snarled.

"You're crazy. I can't do it," Hackensfield said, throwing caution to the wind. "Don't you know what they've done?"

"What have they done?"

"They set about Grantham and Eller. My God! You ought to see those guys. The things they did to them. I tell you we've got to prosecute. The authorities will demand an enquiry. We can't get out of this."

Raven felt a little sick. "You've got to!" he shouted violently. "If you get those girls to testify the balloon goes up. Once they start openin' their mouths they'll never shut them again. The racket'll go sky-high, an' you'll go with it. Listen, Hackensfield, you've got to stop them testifying. I don't care how you do it, but you've got to stop them. Do you understand?"

Hackensfield's voice cracked in his panic. "I tell you we can't do it. Two murders have been committed. The newspapers have got all the details. They'll splash it in every newspaper. The public will demand a trial. This is the most horrible and sensational crime that's ever been committed in this town. You'll have to get the hell out of here and leave it to me to handle. Can't you see that?"

"If you think I'm goin' to pass up nearly a million dollars of investments just because you're too damned milky to stop it, you're crazy. I'll stop it if I have to break into the gaol and shoot every one of those whores. Now do you understand that I mean business?"

There was a pause, then Hackensfield said, "It won't work. Think about it. Statements will be taken from the girls as soon as they get to the station. They'll find out that some of the girls have come from other States. The F.B.I. have already gone down to the station to see if they can horn in on the investigation. We can't keep them out. As soon as they know there are girls from other States they can take charge through the Mann Act. No, it's all up. Every one of us'll have to save his own hide."

Raven hung up and stepped out of the phone booth, trembling with suppressed rage. Hackensfield was right. The thing had come too fast for him to act. The F.B.I. would take over and he'd be on the run again. There wasn't a moment to delay.

He climbed into the taxi and gave Franky's address. He had to pick Maltz up, although by now Franky's wouldn't be safe.

During the drive he took out his wallet and counted the amount of money he had on him. He'd got just over two hundred dollars. When he thought that he could put his hands on nearly a million dollars if he could only get back to the hotel, he shivered with rage and frustration. He'd got to get that money, even if he raided the hotel and took it at the point of a gun.

He paid off the taxi at Franky's and, holding the butt of his gun, walked in.

Maltz, Little Joe and Lefty came across the lobby as soon as they saw him.

"You got a car?" he snapped.

Lefty nodded. "At the back."

"Then let's get out of here," Raven said.

They went through Franky's place and got in the car. "Where to, boss?" Lefty asked.

"Drive around. I want to talk," Raven returned, lighting a cigarette. "Just keep moving."

The car swung away from the kerb.

"Well, what did you find out?" Raven asked Maltz.

Maltz seemed bewildered. "The cops are in your apartment," he said. "They took Sadie away. What the hell's happenin'?"

Raven's face twisted. "It's that rat Grantham," he snarled. "I was crazy to have trusted him. I told him to get rid of Ellinger and he didn't do it. Now Ellinger's finished us."

Little Joe scratched his head. "What do we do now?" he asked. "Shall we beat it out of town?"

Raven shook his head. "Before we go we've got to have some dough. We're goin' to the St. Louis Hotel an' collect the dough I've got in my apartment."

Maltz said patiently, "I told you the cops are in there. They'll have found it by now."

Raven shook his head. "No guy's goin' to open my safe in a few hours. We've got to get that dough, Maltz."

Lefty said, "The G-men will be up there too."

Raven showed his teeth. "Yeah? What of it? We'll go up the back way with Thompsons. They won't have a chance."

The others looked at each other uneasily. "Those guys can shoot," Little Joe said nervously.

Raven nodded. "So can we. St. Louis Hotel, Lefty."

12

September 8th, 6.5 p.m.

Campbell, special agent of the Federal Bureau of Investigation, smiled at Sadie reassuringly. He sat behind a large desk in a severely furnished office.

"Before you give me your evidence," he said, "I'll tell you something about this guy Cruise. For one thing, that's not his name. Fortunately, Mr. Ellinger obtained a perfect set of prints for us. We've had these checked. They belong to a man whom we know as Raven and who we've been looking for for some time. This Raven had a bad criminal record in Chicago. He made things too hot for himself and pulled out. He pulled out in a stolen car and crossed a State line. That gave us a chance of getting after him. We lost sight of him here, although he was reported to have been seen further south. Never mind that. As far as you're concerned, you're safe from him. We shall give you special protection, and until he's rounded up you'll stay out of town with a special guard. You're very important to us. Not only can you prove that he was the guy who killed Mendetta, but your testimony on his Slave racket will get him on the other counts we are bringing against him."

Sadie moved restlessly. "Will it take long?" she asked.

Campbell shrugged. "I don't think so. We mustn't underrate this man. He's clever, and he may still give us the slip, but with your help I think we'll get him quickly. Can you tell me anything about his habits? Did he like movies, for instance? You see, what we have to do in a case like this is to find out everything we can about a wanted man. They have their own little peculiarities. Some of them are crazy about racing. Sooner or later they'll appear on a race-track, and we catch them there. You see what I'm getting at?"

Sadie drew a deep breath. "He was crazy about toy trains," she said.

Campbell lifted his eyebrows. "Now, that's something." He made a note on a pad. "I was goin' to ask about that. We found a big outfit in his rooms."

Sadie nodded. "When he wasn't working he used to make

me set out the tracks and he'd spend hours playing with the trains."

"Anything else?"

Sadie shook her head. "No. Just the trains."

"Did he smoke or drink heavily?"

Again Sadie shook her head. "Just average, I think."

"You've been through a pretty tough time, Mrs. Perminger," Campbell said quietly. "I hate to remind you of some things, but every little help you can give us will make our task less difficult."

Sadie said tonelessly, "I understand."

Taking from his desk drawer a thick portfolio, Campbell selected a large batch of pictures. "Here are photos of girls who have been reported missing during the last three months. I want to see if you can identify any of them. You were in one of the houses for some time and there is a chance that you saw some of them."

Sadie took the batch and went through them slowly. Campbell watched her thoughtfully. It seemed incredible to him that she should be so cold and calm after what she had been through.

She handed him back about thirty photos. "All these girls were one time or another in my house," she said.

"Can you explain how this business was worked?" Campbell asked. "Some of these girls came from Springfield, Cleveland, Denver, and such places. Did they come willingly, or how did he get hold of them?"

Sadie shook her head. "It was all horribly simple. He had special men who were always on the look-out for lonely girls—girls who weren't happy at home; girls who wanted a good time. They had to be pretty and young. When these men found them they either drugged them and took them by car to Sedalia, which was their clearing-post, or else they invented some story about an accident and got them to come that way. The method differed each time, but it was always a quick, simple plan that was unlikely to arouse suspicions."

"Sedalia?" Campbell repeated.

Sadie nodded. "Every girl I spoke to had been taken there."

Campbell reached for his phone and gave some rapid orders. "I'll get that place looked over immediately," he said to

Sadie. "When they got them to Sedalia, what happened then?"

Sadie flinched. "Must I talk about that?"

"I know just how you feel, but if we're to save other girls from this business we must know all about it."

"From what I heard, the girls were put in separate rooms and left to sleep off the drugs. When they recovered they found themselves in bed with a coloured man. It was always a coloured man. Sometimes it was a Chink, or a nigger, or even a Phillipine. They relied on the psychological shock to lower the girl's resistance, and in most cases it was successful. Some of the girls refused, of course, and then they would beat them into submission." Sadie shuddered. "No one knows what that means unless you've actually experienced it. To be beaten every hour of the day until your body is swollen and so tender that the weight of a sheet makes you scream in agony. No one can stand that, Mr. Campbell. I don't care who it is."

Campbell nodded. "I understand," he said.

"When Raven took over he had other methods of subduing girls. He poured turpentine over them. That was worse than the beatings." Sadie put her hand to her eyes. "Mr. Campbell, this man mustn't get away."

"He won't. I promise you that." Campbell got to his feet. "I think that'll do for the moment," he went on. "I'm sending you out of town to a quiet little place where you can rest. I want to congratulate you on your courage. After the things you've told me, it is remarkable that you've stood up to it so well."

Sadie stood looking at him, her face cold and hard. "Do you think I can ever forget?" she said. "My life's ruined. I can't go back to my husband. I can't settle to anything. I want revenge, Mr. Campbell. It may be wicked to say that, but I want to see this Raven suffer as I was made to suffer. Thank God those girls killed Grantham and Eller. If I could do the same to Raven I should die happy."

Under her glance of cold, malicious hatred Campbell turned uneasily away.

13

September 8th, 6.10 p.m.

Lefty parked the car just outside the back entrance of the hotel. There was no one about.

Raven got out of the car. His face was very white. "Get the Thompsons out," he snapped, looking up and down the deserted alley.

Maltz pulled up the back seat and took out three Thompsons. Raven took one and Lefty another.

Little Joe said uneasily, "Shall I stick with the heap?"

Raven shook his head. "We'll want everyone up there," he said grimly. "Don't forget, boys, there's nearly a million bucks in my safe. We split."

"As long as there ain't a million G-men, that'll be fine," Lefty said with a tight smile.

Raven walked quickly into the hotel. The porter, sitting in his little office, gave them a startled look. When he saw the Thompsons his hand went out to the telephone. Raven lifted the long muzzle of the machine-gun.

The porter gave a sickly smile and took his hand away.

Raven said to Lefty, "Fix that bird."

Lefty took two quick steps and the butt of his gun crashed down on the porter's head. The porter slumped down on the floor of his office.

"Fast, now," Raven said, stepping into the elevator.

The others crowded in after him. They were all very nervous. The elevator whined up between the floors.

Raven said, as the cage slid to a standstill, "Gettin' out's goin' to be a picnic. Shoot first an' talk after."

He stepped out of the elevator and began a stiff-legged walk down the corridor.

His suite was round the first bend.

Little Joe took off his hat and wiped his face with his sleeve. This was scaring hell out of him. He clutched his blunt-nose automatic, ready to flop at the first burst of fire.

Raven crept to the bend in the corridor. Every sound was muffled by the heavy carpet. He knew this was sheer madness, but he wasn't going to part with all that dough without a fight. If he got his hands on it he was all right. The thought of once more being on the run, without money, frightened him far more than a hail of lead.

He looked round the bend. Two cops stood in the passage looking towards him. They saw him at the same time as he saw them. He swung up his Thompson and gave them a short burst. The sudden clatter of the gun as it spat lead crashed down the corridor. One of the cops fell forward on his face, but the other darted into Raven's room.

Swearing softly, Raven ran forward, the others following him. The door was open, and Raven paused as he reached it. He had no intention of rushing in. Kneeling down, he swung the muzzle of the gun round the door, spraying lead.

A revolver cracked twice in reply and bullets thudded into the opposite wall. Raven glanced at the wall, saw the angle, which told him the cop was lying down, and lowered the muzzle, firing at the same time.

He heard the cop give a gasp, and he took a chance. He burst into the room, firing wildly. The cop was lying in a pool of blood, the top of his head blown off.

Maltz crowded in and, holding his gun at his hip, ran into the other rooms. There was no one else there.

Raven grinned at him as he came back. "Stand by the door," he said, "while I get the safe open."

He laid his gun down and ran over to the small wall safe. Feverishly he spun the little knob, muttering the combination out loud as he did so.

The others stood in the corridor, tense and expectant.

It took several minutes to open the safe. As he pulled the door open he heard the wailing of sirens in the street. He grabbed two large packets of notes that he knew he'd find there. "I've got 'em," he shouted, picking up his gun. "Come on, let's scram."

Just as he stepped into the corridor the main elevator door opened and several cops spilled out.

Maltz fired on them, falling flat. The cops opened up with a withering fire and Raven only just darted back into the room in time. Stuffing the packets of money inside his coat, he ran into the bathroom and threw up the window. Down below he could see police-cars drawing up outside the hotel and cops crowding out. There were a lot of them. He turned back once more and ran into his bedroom, which looked out on the back alley. He knew there was a fire-escape there.

All the time he could hear the gun-battle raging outside in the corridor. He couldn't think of the others now. They'd have to look after themselves. As he threw up his bedroom window he heard a crash of something exploding and then faintly the smell of pear drops came to him. Tear gas! He swung out on to the fire-escape. It wouldn't be more than minutes before they'd get after him. He raced up the iron stairs. Below him he heard a shout, and then someone started firing at him. Bullets zipped past him, unpleasantly close. As he threw himself blindly over the parapet of the roof one of the packets fell from inside his coat and landed with a little thud on the iron staircase. He knew he couldn't get it. It would mean exposing himself to the fire below. Cursing, he took the other packet and put it inside his shirt, then he ran across the roof top, lowered himself over another parapet, took a stiff drop on to another roof, and ran on again.

Any moment he expected to hear shots behind him. Now that he was on the rim he felt once more the bitter calculating thing of destruction he was before he made money. Every instinct was razor sharp, and even as he climbed across the roofs of the buildings he was already making plans well in advance.

He must get out of town. Stations and roads would be watched. He knew he couldn't get out of town without aid. He thought of the various people whom he had known, and bitterly he was forced to reject each one. There was no one he could turn to. Grantham, Eller, Lefty, Little Joe, Maltz and the rest of them were finished. He knew that. He was on his own now. He didn't mind that. He'd got money. That would always be his best friend.

By now he'd reached the end of the block. Peering round a chimney-stack, he could see the police climbing on to the hotel roof some distance away. They began to move very cautiously towards him. Well, they'd take a little while to catch up at that rate.

By his feet was a trap-door. He lifted it carefully and

lowered himself into an attic room, drawing the trap-door in place after him. He knew the block was by now surrounded. He took the bundle of money out of his shirt and split it into four small packets. These he distributed carefully in each pocket of his suit. It was no use carrying the Thompson any longer. He put it in the corner of the room and then opened the door and walked into a corridor.

As he walked towards the head of the stairs he loosened his automatic in its shoulder-holster. The place seemed to be a block of offices. When he reached the second landing, rows of frosted-panelled doors confirmed this. At the end of the corridor he saw a gentleman's toilet. He hesitated a moment and then went in.

The only occupant was a window-cleaner, who was leaning out of the window. Raven eyed his uniform and realized his chance.

The window-cleaner, hearing him come in, looked over his shoulder. "Seems like there's a lotta excitement poppin' at the St. Louis," he said with a grin. "The place is lousy with cops."

Raven came to the window and looked down. A heavy cordon had been thrown round the block and the street was packed with interested sight-seers.

"What's it all about?" he asked, stepping back.

"Search me," the window-cleaner returned, still looking down into the street. "Some excitement."

Raven drew his automatic and let the barrel slide into his hand, then he dealt the window-cleaner a crushing blow at the back of his head.

14

September 9th, 10.25 a.m.

Jay Ellinger walked into the F.B.I. offices and asked for Campbell. He was shown up immediately.

Campbell got up from behind his desk and shook hands. "Sit down, Ellinger," he said, pushing over a box of cigars. "Make yourself at home."

Jay shook his head at the cigars. "Too early for me,

thanks," he said, taking out his cigarette-case. "I just looked in to hear how things were going."

Campbell smiled. "You're free, ain't you?" he said. "I mean, you're lookin' for some sort of job?"

Jay looked surprised. "Why, sure," he said, "I guess I am."

"Ever thought anythin' about this racket?"

"What? A Federal Agent?"

Campbell nodded. "I've been on to Mr. Hoover's chief of staff. We think you'd make a good agent, Ellinger."

"Why, sure," Jay said eagerly, "I'd jump at it."

"Seeing that it was through your efforts this big Slave Ring's been exposed, we thought it only fair to let you in at the death. What do you say?"

"It's mighty nice of you."

"Okay, then I'll fix it. A Federal Agent has to sit for all sorts of examinations and has to go through all kinds of tests and training before he can join up. I'm goin' to let you off these for the time being. You'll work with one of my operators and you'll just be his assistant. When we've cleaned all this business up you'll be posted to one of our trainin' centres. Right now there isn't the time for it."

Jay nodded. "That's fine. You can rely on me to do as I'm told. I'd like to see the end of this guy Raven."

"So you shall." Campbell pressed a bell. "I'll get Hogarty to come in."

A moment later a tall, thick-set man entered. "Mornin", Chief," he said, tipping his hat.

"Hogarty, meet Jay Ellinger. You've heard about him. I'm sending Ellinger along with you. He might be able to help. When all this is over he's being sworn in."

Hogarty shook hands with Jay. He seemed pleased to know him. "You've done a smart bit of work already," he observed.

"Okay. Now what've you to report?" Campbell asked, signing Hogarty to another chair.

Hogarty sat down. "Well, Chief, he's got away. I'm sorry about it, but somehow or other he slipped through the cordon."

Campbell shrugged. "I didn't expect it to be that easy," he said. "He can't leave town, can he?"

"He'll be damn clever if he does," Hogarty said grimly. "The place is sewed up tight enough."

"What about the other guys?"

"Two of them are dead, and Little Joe's ready to squawk."

Campbell nodded. "You better see he's put somewhere where they can't get at him," he said. "What about Mrs. Perminger... she all right?"

"Yeah. We've got her out in the country. I've put three operators on to her and she's got a woman to keep her company. She'll be right on the spot when the guy comes to trial. Jeeze! Does she hate that fella?"

Campbell's face hardened. "She's got a lot of reasons for hatin' him," he said. "It beats me how she came through at all."

Hogarty climbed to his feet. "Women are tough," he said. "And when a dame hates like that Mrs. P., I'd sooner be a long way away from her."

"What are you goin' to do now?"

"Stick around. It takes time, Chief. If he's run to ground we'll have to wait for him. Sooner or later he'll make a slip an' then we'll get him."

"You're sure the town's sewed up?"

"It's tight. Every road's bein' watched. The stations are looking out for him and the airport too. No, I guess he'll have to stay out. It's a pity he got away with all that dough. It makes things much easier when they're broke."

"All right, take Ellinger along with you. Get after him, Hogarty; we want quick results."

Hogarty jerked his head to Ellinger. "Sure," he said, and as they went out he winked at Jay. "Maybe he does want quick results, but he ain't goin' to get them," he told Jay as they walked down the passage. "Sometimes it takes months before a guy breaks from cover. We just have to wait."

Jay followed him out into the crowded street.

15

September 9th, 10.45 a.m.

On the third floor of a shabby little hotel Raven slept behind the locked door of the grimy bedroom he had rented. He slept uneasily. A gun lay beside him on the soiled sheet. He hadn't taken off his clothes. Newspapers covered the floor so that anyone approaching his bed would, by the rustle of the papers, wake him.

He wore a smart black suit that the hotel owner had obtained for him. The hotel owner was a guy called Goshawk. Raven had paid him well and he hadn't asked questions. Already he knew who Raven was. Everywhere pictures of Raven proclaimed him as a wanted man. As long as he continued to pay Goshawk he knew he was safe, but he knew that if he was to make his get-away and have enough to start some other racket he couldn't stay long. Goshawk knew how to charge.

Raven stirred uneasily and then sat up quickly. His hand closed round the gun as he listened. He heard nothing, and relaxed.

The four grimy walls of the room oppressed him. He wanted to get up and go out, but he knew he daren't do that. Even from his bedroom window he could see a poster on a hoarding carrying his photograph. The F.B.I. weren't taking any chances with him.

He swung his legs over the side of the bed and got up. He glanced at the clock. It didn't matter to him what time it was, he'd got no place to go.

Moving across to the wash-basin, he bathed his face and decided to shave. While taking his collar and tie off he happened to look across the road at an opposite house. He stood still staring.

A girl, dressed in a white flimsy step-in, was wandering backwards and forwards in front of the window. She seemed to be doing a dance routine. By listening carefully he could hear the faint strains of a gramophone.

Keeping carefully out of sight, he stood watching her. His first reaction was that she'd be a good type for one of his houses, then his second reaction was a sudden forgotten lust that made him want her as he had never wanted a woman before.

She was medium height, with a mass of corn-coloured curls. Even from where he was standing he could see she had an exceptionally good figure. She drifted round the room smoothly, and then, as the record came to an end, she disappeared from view.

Thoughtfully Raven picked up his shaving-brush and began to lather his face. He kept his eyes fixed on the window. It was only when he'd finished shaving that she reappeared. This time she was dressed in a red-and-white-spotted dress, and she came out on the little iron balcony and looked down into the street.

Raven could see a lot more of her. Again he felt a pang go through him. A tap at the door startled him and he growled, "Who is it?" laying his hand on the gun.

"Goshawk."

He crossed the room and unlocked the door.

Goshawk came in with a tray. He was a little scraggy man with hard gimlet eyes and a heavily dyed moustache. He set the tray down on the bed.

Raven took him by his arm and pulled him to the window. "Who's that dame?" he asked.

Goshawk stared and shook his head. "Search me," he said indifferently. "Why?"

"Never mind why," Raven snarled. "Find out at once. Send someone over to that house and find out who she is. I don't care how you do it, and don't make anyone suspicious, but find out." He gave him a twenty-dollar bill. "Ten more if you get what I want."

Goshawk shook his head. "Make it another twenty," he said.

Raven, his face going white with fury, seized him by his scraggy neck. "You down-at-heel louse," he said furiously; "you try an' twist me an' see what comes to you."

Goshawk backed away hurriedly. He felt his throat tenderly with his grimy hand. "All right, Mr. Raven," he said, touching his forehead with a long bony finger.

Raven said through his teeth, "Don't call me that!"

Goshawk backed away and went out of the room. Raven locked the door after him and then went to the window. The girl had gone.

He turned back to his breakfast. A newspaper lay on the top of the tray, folded in such a way that his photo stared up at him. He picked up the paper savagely and tossed it across the room.

He had no appetite for his breakfast, and after a few mouthfuls he pushed the tray away and lit a cigarette. How was he to get out of this place? Everywhere his picture reminded the crowded streets to look for him. He went over to the mirror and stared at himself. If he grew a moustache and dyed his hair he might get some place. He could wear tinted glasses too. Yes, that was it. He found himself quivering with excitement. Goshawk would have to help him, but then Goshawk would know of his disguise. A cruel smile came to the thin lips. Maybe Goshawk would have a little accident.

16

September 9th, 11.45 a.m.

Goshawk said, "I found out about the dame over the way. Her name's Marie Leroy. She's flat broke an' wants to go to Hollywood. Thinks she's a dancer. She's an orphan, and can't get a job. At the end of the week she'll be told to dust."

Raven lit a cigarette. His fireplace was littered with stubs. "What's she goin' to do?"

Goshawk shrugged. "I'll tell you what she won't do," he said with a sly smile. "She won't decorate no guy's bed. That kind of a dame is a so-far-and-no-mother dame."

Raven sneered. "That's what you think," he said. "Given the opportunity, the time, and if you kid 'em enough, it's a cinch with any dame."

"Yeah?" Goshawk shook his head. "You ain't thinkin' of havin' a try, are you? I shouldn't have thought your mind was on dames. You've got your hands full, ain't you?"

Raven ignored him. He got up from the rickety armchair. "I want you to get me a pair of tinted eye-glasses," he said, "an' some bleachin' stuff for my hair."

Goshawk's eyes narrowed. "Thinkin' of pullin' outta here?"

"Nope. Just makin' myself look different."

"Okay, I'll get 'em," and he went out.

When he had gone, Raven turned away savagely. He knew that as soon as he stopped paying the rat dough he'd squeal. That type always did. All right, when he was ready to pull out he'd fix him.

He went and sat by his window, keeping just behind the

dirty white curtain, and looked across at Marie Leroy's room.
The empty window made him more lonely than he'd ever felt,
and he just sat there smoking, waiting for her to come back.

When Goshawk brought him his lunch he was still sitting
there. A pair of tinted glasses and a bottle of peroxide was also
on the tray.

Raven ate his meal moodily, every now and then glancing
at the window. His active mind was already making plans. After
lunch he sat down and wrote a letter. He spent some time in
composing it, and when he had finished he sat back and read it
through.

Dear Miss Leroy,
I understand you are interested in a chance to get to
Hollywood. I'm going there myself. Shall we go together? I've got
a car and the expense of the trip is in my hands. This is entirely
a business proposition and I'm asking you to accompany me on
the trip as it is essential for me to travel with someone like
yourself. I'll explain more fully when I meet you, which I propose
to do in a few days' time.
Yours sincerely,
James Young.

He put the letter in an envelope and put it on the tray.
When Goshawk came to take the tray away he told him to mail
it.

"Whorin' by mail now, huh?" Goshawk said.

"Do what you're told, an' shut your trap," Raven snarled at
him.

When Goshawk had gone he set about bleaching his hair.
It took time, but when he'd finished the result in the mirror
startled him. It certainly altered his appearance. He tried on his
glasses. It still wasn't good enough. With a moustache it would
be better. All right, he'd raise a moustache. It wouldn't take him
long. He felt the little bristles already growing on his top lip.

He sat on the edge of his bed and thought. Today was
Tuesday. Tomorrow she'd get the letter. At the end of the week
she'd have to leave her room. It ought to work. She was up

against it. This was a chance right in her lap. Thursday night he'd go across and see her. Friday night they'd go. In the meantime he'd got to get a better suit and he'd got to get a car. How the hell was he going to do that? If Goshawk knew he was pulling out, would he keep his trap shut until he was gone, or would he yap at once? If Raven promised to pay him a lump sum if he got away safely he'd have to keep silent. Yes, that was what he'd have to do.

Tomorrow he'd get Goshawk to arrange about the car. He'd have to steal some spare plates. He sat there making his plans until the room grew dim in the evening light, then, remembering, he wandered over to the window. Across the way she had come in and had put on the light. He sat down and watched her behind the curtain. She didn't dance that night, but sat limply in a chair, staring at the opposite wall, as lonely and as dejected as Raven himself.

17

September 10th, 10.15 a.m.

Raven regarded himself in the mirror. He saw reflected there a thin, well-dressed man, whose eyes were hidden behind dark glasses. His hair and slight moustache were almost white. It wasn't the Raven he knew. He was confident that no one could possibly recognize him.

He drew a deep breath.

"You look pretty good," Goshawk said, looking at him. "I guess you could walk past any cop an' get away with it."

Raven nodded. "I'll be tryin' in a few days," he said.

Goshawk gave a little snigger. "I'd like to be there to see it," he said. "Yeah, I certainly would like to be there to see it."

Both men smiled. Both men had their own secret thoughts, only Raven knew what was in Goshawk's mind. It was only by exerting tremendous self-control that he didn't smash his fist into Goshawk's face there and then.

When Goshawk had gone he went to the window. He felt strangely excited. Marie Leroy was getting ready to go out. She was adjusting a little hat in front of her mirror.

He hesitated no longer. Crossing the room, he opened the door and went downstairs. In the street he took several deep breaths. It meant a lot to him after being cooped up in that one little room. Then he hurriedly walked to the end of the street.

A policeman came sauntering past him, and Raven felt a little tightness round his chest as he passed. The policeman took no notice of him and at the corner of the street Raven stopped and turned.

Marie Leroy had just come out of her house and was walking towards him. He liked the way she walked. She took long, graceful steps and her body swung in harmony. He could see her breasts under the thin covering of her dress jerk a little as she moved. There was no doubt she was a honey all right.

He advanced towards her and as she drew level he raised his hat. The sun reflected on his pale silvery hair. "Miss Leroy?" he said. "My name's Young—James Young."

She stared at him. He could see she had very blue eyes. Then she said, "Oh yes," and stood looking at him.

His thin lips smiled. "I guess you think I'm a little crazy, but I ain't. You got my letter, didn't you?"

"Yes. I don't know what to make of it."

"We can't talk in the street. There's a coffee-shop further along here. May we go there?"

He turned and began to move along the street. She fell into step beside him. He nearly laughed. It was a push-over.

"My letter may have been a bit mysterious," he said. "But when I explain, you can see how absurdly simple it is. Before we go any further, I'd like you to know that I'm a director of Lazard Film Company. I've just been back here to look up my old folks. I'm returning to Hollywood on Friday."

He saw her eyes sparkle. "Gee!" she said. "You really mean you direct films?"

He nodded. "Yeah, an' believe me it's a lousy job."

They entered the cafe and sat down. He ordered coffee and crackers.

"Now let me explain. I've got myself hooked up to an absurd bet, and I'm wantin' you to help me out. It's like this. One of the guys back in Hollywood was saying that every girl in the States wanted to be an actress. I told him he was crazy. So we got into an argument and one thing led to another until somehow or other I betted him that I could stop the first girl I met and could bring her back to Hollywood, and she wouldn't want to be an actress. Do you follow me?"

Marie Leroy nodded, her blue eyes puzzled.

"Well, sister, believe it or not, every girl I've asked so far wants to be an actress. Well, I've quit tryin'. I've gotta go back on Friday an' I'll have to say I was licked. Well, it sticks, sister. I don't like admittin' I'm licked. So I'm thinkin' I'll cheat a little. I heard from a guy that you want to go out there and you want to be a dancer. Okay, I'll take you there if you want to go, if you'll first of all come to see my boy friend and tell him you want to dance and not act. And if you do this I'll see you get in one of the dancin' troupes down there."

She said, "You wouldn't be kiddin', because if you are you're playin' an awful mean game."

Raven shook his head. "I'm not kiddin'. Why so serious, sister? Are things goin' badly for you?"

She nodded. "I guess they are," she said, looking out of the window at the crowded street beyond. "I'm broke flat and nowhere to go."

"Looks like your lucky day," Raven said, feeling the blood surging through his veins. "Is it a bet?"

"It's business, isn't it?" she said.

Raven nearly laughed in her face. What the hell did she think? If she thought he was going to drive her half across America and not give her a tumble she was crazy.

"You don't have to worry about that angle," he assured her. "You won't have any complaints."

She played with the handle of her spoon. "You don't mind if I'm straight with you, do you, Mr. Young?"

Raven shook his head. "I'd like it."

"I want to go. In fact, it is the chance I've been dreaming about, but it's too good to be true. I feel there's a catch in it somewhere."

"There isn't, but if you feel nervous about it, I won't press you."

She looked at him as if trying to read his mind. She didn't like the cold eyes or the thin mouth, but she knew she'd go. She couldn't afford to do anything else. She had to get to Hollywood.

She said, "Well, thanks, I'll go, anyway. Don't think I'm

ungrateful, but a girl's got to be careful."

Raven nodded. "It does me a lotta good to see you hesitate," he said. "Some of the dames I've spoken to would have thrown in a lot of things to come with me. I don't like that type of dame." He finished his coffee and stood up. "Friday night about nine-thirty. I'll pick you up. Don't bring too much baggage, will you?"

He didn't offer to shake hands. Out in the street he raised his hat. "Thanks a lot for helping me out, Miss Leroy."

He watched her walk away and then he returned to his room. With a dame like that at his side, and a good car, his changed appearance, he'd get out of town. He wouldn't even bother to sneak out. He was confident that he could go by the main streets and even wave to the Feds as he passed them.

18

September 13th, 9 p.m.

The night was very hot and the moon rode high in tattered clouds.

Raven paced slowly backwards and forwards in his room. He had carefully drawn the blinds, and now he waited for the first step in his escape. In a few minutes Goshawk would come up. Around at the back was a two-seater car that had cost Raven plenty, waiting to take him to liberty. No one knew about his changed appearance except Goshawk. Raven's thin face twisted a little.

He heard steps coming down the passage, and from force of habit his hand slid inside his coat, gripping his gun.

Goshawk knocked and Raven let him in. The two men looked at each other.

"So you're off?" Goshawk said. "Takin' the little dame with you?"

Raven controlled his face. This guy knew all the answers. He shook his head. "Car outside?"

"Sure!"

"Is she full?"

"Yeah. Take you a couple of hundred miles, if you ain't stopped before then." Goshawk sniggered.

Raven sat down on the bed. "Well, I guess I'll settle up with you," he said. He took out a small roll from his side pocket that he had specially prepared for Goshawk. "Let's see, I've paid for the car and for a month's rent. I'll make you a present of that. Then I guess you'll want a little consideration for keepin' your trap shut, won't you?"

Goshawk rubbed his hands. "They're offering five grand for information that'll lead to your arrest."

Raven stiffened. "Five grand?" he repeated, staring at Goshawk.

"That's right. A nice slice of change, ain't it?"

Raven almost laughed. The fool had signed his own death warrant. No matter how much Raven gave him now, he'd squeal as soon as he could get to the cops. Five grand was too much money to pass up.

Raven got off the bed. "If I give you the same, you'll be happy, won't you?"

Goshawk's little eyes glittered. "Sure," he said. "That's fair enough."

Raven took another roll out of his pocket. "You'll find five grand here, I think. Count it." He put the roll into Goshawk's trembling hands and wandered away to the window. He lifted the blind a trifle and glanced over at Marie's room. He could see her moving about the room hurriedly. He guessed she was packing. Time was getting on. He glanced over at Goshawk, who sat on the bed counting the notes.

Drawing his gun and holding it by the barrel, he approached Goshawk. "You've got enough dough there to make you rich," he said casually, coming closer step by step.

Goshawk nodded, muttering figures as he laid the bills down on the bed. Raven was right behind him, and he swung his arm. Goshawk suddenly cringed and he gave a thin little cry of terror as he saw Raven's shadow on the soiled sheet, the upraised arm coming down and the gun, looking three times its size, in the big distorted hand.

The gun-butt cracked his skull and he fell across the bed, blood and brains oozing out of a hole that appeared suddenly in his head.

Raven stepped back hastily. He knew he didn't have to strike again. The blow had jarred his hand and arm badly. He stood looking down at Goshawk, a feeling of relief surging through him. The one man who knew enough to have him burnt was silenced for ever. Now he was free. All he had to do was to walk out, get in the car, pick up the Leroy dame and beat it.

He dragged Goshawk further on to the bed and covered him with a blanket. Anyone looking in the room would think that Raven was there, sleeping. He covered the head with a pillow and then he paused to light a cigarette. He glanced at the clock. It was twenty past nine. All was working satisfactorily. As he turned to the door his eye alighted on the wall calendar.

FRIDAY, 13th SEPTEMBER

It made him pause.

"My lucky day," he said with a forced laugh, and went out, locking the door and removing the key.

He met no one as he went downstairs. He let himself out the back way and at the end of the alley he found the big Chrysler waiting for him. He climbed in and started the engine. He could hardly believe that he was off, that he had a fast car under him, and that in a few hours St. Louis would be a long way behind.

He drove round the block once, and as the hands of a street clock moved to the half-hour, he drew up outside Marie Leroy's apartment house.

She was standing in the hallway waiting, and as he drew up she picked up two handbags and ran down the steps. He made no effort to get out. From where he sat he could see people peering round curtains all down the street. He wasn't going to let them give his description to the cops if anyone got suspicious.

"Can you manage?" he called. "The bags can go in the boot behind. It's quite easy to open. My engine's cold. I've got to nurse her along for a minute."

"That's all right," she said, and he felt two thuds as the bags were dumped in the back. Leaning over, he opened the off-door and she got in. She wore the same red-and-white-spotted dress, and as she sat down the skirt rode up. Her long tapering legs sent a little shiver through him. She pulled her skirt down and laughed nervously. "Some car," she said.

"Like it?" He engaged the gears. "We've got a mighty long way to go. I've been sleepin' all the afternoon an' I want to get as far as I can tonight."

She relaxed back against the upholstered seat. "I like

driving at night. When you get tired may I drive?"

He looked at her. "Can you?"

"Of course."

This was something he hadn't thought of. If they took it in turns to sleep and drive they'd halve the time.

"That's fine," he said, and meant it.

He drove steadily, keeping to an even forty miles an hour. He had no wish to get an excited speed cop on his trail. Goshawk had given him forged licence papers, but even with those he wasn't going to take chances.

As they neared the outskirts of the town Marie said, "Look, there's a barricade ahead. How exciting! You'll have to stop."

Raven eased the gun loose in its shoulder-holster and stopped the car a few feet from the swinging red light.

Three State troopers came up to the car. Two of them carried Thompsons.

Raven felt his mouth go dry, but he kept his head.

Marie leant out of the window. "What is it?" she asked.

They played a powerful light on her and then turned it on Raven, who had quickly removed his hat. "What's the trouble, officer?" he asked. "I wasn't goin' too fast, was I?"

"Let's have a look at your papers, buddy," the State trooper said, resting his foot on the running-board. Raven noticed that the other two troopers had relaxed and were no longer pointing their guns at him.

He produced his papers. "Here you are," he said.

Marie seemed to be getting on well with the other two troopers. Raven couldn't hear what she was saying as she was leaning out of the window, but one of the troopers laughed suddenly and he heard her laugh too.

Hardly glancing at the licence papers, the trooper returned them. "Your wife, I guess?" he asked.

Raven nodded.

"Okay, bud, on your way."

Raven engaged his gears and the car slid past the barricade. A sudden thought had struck him. He'd got to be damn careful with this girl. What a fool he'd been not to have remembered!

She said excitedly, "They're looking for Public Enemy No. 1. A man called Raven. He's supposed to be hiding in the town.

Isn't it exciting?"

"Yeah," he said, with a little grin, "but I've got some news for you that'll startle you. I was crazy to have brought you, sister."

Her eyes opened. "Why?"

He continued to drive. "Ever heard of the Mann Act?"

"Why, yes? What's that got to do with it?"

"Plenty. It's an offence to take any dame but your wife over a State line. There's a twenty-years rap hanging to it."

Marie's eyes opened. "But—but they let us through."

Raven's mouth twitched. "Yeah—I told 'em you were my wife. The car, the clothes and the general set-up passed us."

There was a long pause. Then Raven said, "Unless you agree to bein' my wife on this trip, we'd better turn round."

Marie stared straight in front of her. Then she said bitterly, "I might have guessed I'd have to pay one way or another for a trip like this."

Raven put his foot on the brake and the car came to a standstill. "Say the word, sister, and back we go."

She looked at him and shook her head. "It's okay. I dare say it won't kill me," she said, and settled once more comfortably.

Raven sent the car shooting forward. He knew it was in the bag now.

Neither of them spoke for some time. The Chrysler tore through the night, ripping miles off the State Highway. As the hands of the dashboard clock crept on the night grew colder. Both of them began to feel stiff and chilly.

Raven said, "Just ahead is Williamsburg. I guess we'll stop there for a drink."

Marie rubbed her bare arms. "I'll get a coat out when we get there," she said.

In ten minutes they reached the town and Raven stopped the car outside a small all-wood hotel. He went round to the boot and helped her get out a light dust-coat. He also took out a rug.

They went into the hotel together. The clock was just striking a quarter to twelve. They went into a deserted lobby and ordered coffee and rum from a startled negro waiter.

"Tired?" Raven asked, as they sipped the steaming coffee.

She shook her head. "We'll go on." She was very decided about it. Raven grinned to himself.

They got up to go when they had finished. She said, "Shall I drive?"

He nodded. "Sure, if you want to. We'll go on to Columbia, then maybe we'll get some sleep."

She bit her lip. "Couldn't you sleep now? Then we could drive all the time."

"So we could," he said. "You're sure in a hurry to get there, ain't you?"

And he followed her out to the car.

19

September 14th, 11.10 a.m.

Hogarty said, "Think it's Raven?"

Jay and he stared down at the battered Goshawk. Two cops who stood in the room watched them with bored eyes. They never had much use for Federal Agents.

Jay shrugged. "It might be."

"Let's go over the ground again," Hogarty said, turning from the bed. "The girl downstairs says that the guy who had this room never went out. Goshawk always took up his meals. No one else in the hotel ever saw him. That points to Raven, don't it?"

Again Jay shrugged. "Maybe," he said.

"Then the girl over the way. How does she fit in?"

"Suppose we talk to the kid again?"

They went downstairs, where a round-eyed maid stood waiting. Hogarty jerked his head. "Come inside here, sister, an' let's go through with it again. Your name's Alice Cohen, ain't it?"

The girl nodded.

"Your boss sent you across to the apartment house opposite to ask after a certain Marie Leroy—right?"

Again she nodded.

"Well, go on."

"He wanted to find out who she was. The landlady told me. She was a dancer who wanted to go to Hollywood."

"Why should this guy Goshawk want to know that?"

"I don't know. He didn't say."

"You never saw the guy who had that room?"

"No, but Mr. Goshawk sent me out for some tinted spectacles and a bottle of hair bleach. He didn't use them himself. I got to thinking they were for this fella who had the room."

Hogarty and Jay exchanged glances.

"I see," Hogarty said. "Anythin' else."

"I heard Mr. Goshawk arrange about buying a Chrysler car. I was surprised, because Mr. Goshawk was always tight with his dough. I thought he was steppin' out a bit."

"All right, baby, you're doin' fine." Hogarty was excited. "I'll talk to you again in a while. Just stick around."

When she had gone he turned to Jay excitedly. "It looks like it. The troopers at the west barricade report that a blond guy with his wife passed through in a two-seater Chrysler." He checked himself from a note-book. "They say the girl was wearing a red dress with pinhead white spots. Let's go over an' find out if that's the dress this Leroy dame was wearing. If it is, we'll get after them. They're heading for Hollywood by the U.S. Highway 40."

Jay followed him out of the hotel.

20

September 14th, 11.50 p.m.

Raven said, "We'll stop at Odessa for the night."

Marie clenched her fists, but said nothing. The continuous driving had unnerved both of them, and Raven had lost patience. He wasn't going to drive like this day and night, with her sitting at his side. What the hell did she think? She wasn't just goin' to sit around all day and all night, letting him take her free of expense all the way to Hollywood. It was time she paid for her trip.

"It's a tough little town," he said, "but it'll do for the night. We'll stop again at Kansas City. You'll like that."

She said, "It'll take us weeks to get to Hollywood."

"Not after tonight it won't," he said with a little grin. "Time'll go fast enough after tonight."

She looked at him uneasily, but said nothing. A few minutes later they drove into Odessa.

Raven stopped at a petrol station and had his tank filled. He asked where a hotel was, and then drove in the direction indicated.

As they got out of the car he said, "Mr. and Mrs. Young, baby, an' don't forget it."

She walked into the lobby without answering. A negro came out at a run and took their bags. Raven went over and signed the register. The clerk blotted the ink, looked at the name, gave a little start, and glanced up at Raven searchingly.

"Anythin' wrong?" Raven asked, his eyes suddenly going hard.

The clerk shook his head. "Quite okay, sir," he said. "You've omitted to say where you've come from."

Raven took up the pen and scribbled "Jefferson City", then he turned away.

"A double room?" the clerk asked.

Marie stiffened.

"Sure," Raven said, smiling at her. "An' a double bed."

There was no elevator, and they followed the negro up two flights of stairs.

"These hick hotels give me a pain," Raven said.

Marie found she couldn't answer him. Her heart was beating wildly, and she felt a little sick.

They went into a large, shabbily furnished room. The big iron double bed took up a lot of room. When the negro got his tip he left them with a broad grin.

Raven took off his hat and dust-coat and yawned. "How do you like it?" he asked, looking round.

"I think it's horribly sordid," Marie said with a little shudder. "Mr. Young, must we go through with this? You could have given me a single room, couldn't you?"

Raven grinned at her. "Sure I could."

"You said it was business. You said I didn't have anything to worry about. Can't you see this is all horribly sordid?"

Raven sat on the bed. "I've brought you so far," he said, "and I guess I'm entitled to a little consideration from you. But

I won't force myself on you. I'll put it like this. If you want to go on with me you'll stay here tonight and be nice. If you want either to stay in this burg an' rot or walk back to St. Louis, then I'll go off now an' take the car an' leave you to it. What's it to be?"

She said, "Oh, all right. You've got me where you want me, haven't you? I trade my body for the ride. That's what you mean, isn't it?"

Raven's face twitched. "I thought of lettin' you down easy," he said between his teeth, "but if you're goin' to swap smart cracks you'll go the whole way."

She sat on the other side of the bed away from him and began to cry. "My God!" she said. "I've been a fool."

He suddenly lost patience with her and pushed her on to the bed. She saw the sudden lust that had come into his eyes and for a moment a scream hovered in her throat.

Raven said, "Don't yell." He pinched her jaw between two fingers. "Do you want to go through with this or shall I beat it?"

She lay flat on her back and looked up at him. She saw the blank lustful look that made him almost animal.

She could see the little beads of sweat standing out on his toad-coloured skin. She could see his body trembling and she could feel the vibrations shaking the bed. She wanted to say no, but she knew he'd have no mercy on her. He'd leave her here. She had one dollar and forty cents in her purse. What could she do with that?

So she shut her eyes, blotting out the strange inhuman face so close to hers, and through dry lips she told him to go ahead.

He put his hand on the front of her dress and ripped it. The thin material tore easily. She half sat up, but he shoved her down again. "Stay still," he said, his eyes blazing savagely. "I'll buy you everything you want. Stay still."

"No, not like this," she said, taking his wrist in both hands as he gripped her slip. "Please—it's horrible. Not like this."

"Let go. Do you hear? Let go."

Her hands dropped away as he ripped the silk from her and the hot night air slid over her frightened nakedness. She put both her hands over her eyes and began to cry.

Her long white body and her tight drawn-up breasts inflamed him. He reached out two shaking hands towards her, when a heavy rap sounded on the door.

For a second Raven stood paralysed. Then his instinct overrode his lust and he jerked up, his hand pulling his gun from its holster.

"What is it?" he said. His voice sounded cracked and hoarse to him.

Marie half turned on her side, hiding her head in her arms. Her white shoulders heaved with her crying.

"Come on out, Raven, with your hands in the air," someone called.

Raven turned very cold. His mind sprang to the clerk and the start he'd given when he had signed the book. He was trapped. He hadn't even the Thompson, which, like the crazy fool he was, he'd left in the boot of the car. He fired one shot that crashed through the door and he heard footsteps move hastily away.

Marie sat up on the bed with a scream. "What is it?" she said, staring at his gun. "Why are you—shooting? What—"

Raven turned on her savagely. "Shut up!" he snarled.

"Hi, Raven," someone called again, "you can't get away. The place's surrounded. Better give up. You've got no chance in the world."

"Come an' get me!" he shouted back savagely, sending another shot through the door.

"Raven?" Marie gasped. "Are you Raven?"

He turned on her. "Yeah. Now you know, you stupid little bitch. You got me outta town, do you understand? Now, by God, you'll get me out of here too!"

Shoving his gun into his side pocket, he grabbed her by her arm and pulled her to her feet. He wrenched off the ripped clothes that hung on her.

She was too terrified to feel her shame. "What are you going to do with me?" she said.

"You're goin' out there," Raven told her, pulling his gun out again. "You're goin' to walk in front of me. If they shoot at me it's goin' to be too bad for you."

"You can't do that. It's not my fight. You wouldn't force me into this... please... not like this!"

Twisting her arms behind her, he gripped her two wrists in one of his hands, then, crouching close behind her, he shoved her to the door.

"I'm comin' out!" he yelled. "Don't shoot. I'm comin' out."

In a low, savage voice, he said to her, "If you faint, or try any tricks I'll spread your goddamn' guts all over the town." He rammed the cold gun into her backbone, making her cry out with the pain, then he unlocked the door and pushed her out.

The two Federal Agents were so startled when Marie suddenly appeared that for a moment they hesitated. It was that moment that Raven had gambled on. He fired twice almost as one shot. The flash of the gun burnt Marie's arm and she screamed wildly.

The two Agents slowly folded up, one of them shot through the head and the other in the middle of his chest.

Raven said, "Keep moving."

He ran her along the passage, but there was no one about. They went downstairs. At the bottom of the stairs the night clerk lurked, staring up with terrified eyes.

The sight of Marie's naked body seemed to mesmerize him. Raven shot him between the eyes.

He shoved Marie down the stairs fast and they crossed the deserted lobby. Through the open door he could see the Chrysler still parked outside. Another car stood near it, but it was empty.

His brain worked swiftly. The clerk would have reported to the Federal Field Office that he'd come to the hotel. The Feds would send out the alarm and then come on over. In a town like Odessa it was nearly a safe bet that there were only two Feds. The talk of surrounding the place was bluff.

Cautiously he pushed Marie out into the street. No one fired at him. Taking a deep breath, he ran her across to the car. "Get inside," he snarled. "Quick."

She pulled open the door and climbed in. Raven looked over his shoulder, saw something move in the shadows, fired once and then scrambled under the wheel. Desperately he trod on the starter, and as the engine sprang into life he set the car bounding forward.

Marie sat crouched away from him, covering her breasts with her arms and shivering as the cold wind bit into her body.

"Sit still and hold your trap," Raven said, "or I'll finish you."

He knew it was too risky to go on to Kansas and he turned off on to the dirt road that led to Fayetteville. The needle of the speedometer climbed until it stood at 65. On a dirt road that was fast enough. As he drove his mind crawled with schemes. His hair no longer afforded him a disguise. They must be on to that. God! These Federal dicks were smart. If he could only put enough miles between them before they reached Odessa he might stand a chance of beating them. Otherwise it would mean a show-down.

Marie said in a low voice, "Can't you stop a moment? I'm freezin'."

"I'd rather you freeze than me burn," he said with a savage laugh. "Sit on the floor, it's warmer down there. I ain't stoppin' for no one."

She slid off her seat and crouched down on the floorboards. "Can't you let me go?" she pleaded. "I'm no use to you now."

He considered this, then decided to take her a little further. "You shut up," he said. "I don't want another yap outta you."

The road improved as the car ate up the miles, and he was able to increase his speed. He swung through Fayetteville at a terrific speed, and headed south again.

He knew he'd got a tank full of petrol, and with luck he ought to shake them. After a few miles he slowed down and got out.

He said to Marie, "If you move I'll shoot you."

He ran round to the boot and opened it, pulling the Thompson out. He hesitated about taking out one of her bags, then slammed the boot to. To hell with it, he wasn't going to waste time on her.

He stood looking back into the darkness. Far away he could make out two pin-points of light. He knew what they were at once. A car was coming at a great speed. It might not be the Feds, but it was too risky to take chances.

He ran back to the car and climbed in, putting the Thompson behind his head along the top of the seat.

He started the car again and drove off at a furious pace. He glanced at the clock on the dashboard. It showed 2.30. Somehow or other he'd got to get under cover before daylight. He'd got to ditch the car and he'd got to get another. He looked down at Marie, who seemed to have fallen into a doze. He'd got to get rid of her.

His mouth tightened. It was tough on her, but she'd have to

go for good. The pin-points of light were no nearer. He could see them dancing in his rear mirror. They must be three or four miles away. Maybe they could see his own headlights. He hesitated, then reached forward and turned them out. The road, down which he was roaring, suddenly disappeared and he automatically eased up on the accelerator. He sat forward to peer into the darkness. This wasn't going to help his speed, but at the same time he wasn't showing himself to the Feds.

Ahead of him he could just make out a turning; he swung the car, braking as he did so. It was quite a narrow road, bordered by tall trees. He forced the car forward again, gaining speed. There was a good chance that the pursuing car would go on past. They might think he was heading for the State Highway again, which he knew linked up the road he'd been on previously.

He glanced back and then he felt the car run off the road. Instinctively he jammed on his brakes, but he was too late. The car crashed against some trees with such violence that he was nearly shot through the wind-screen.

Marie woke with a start and gave a little scream. Raven climbed out of the wrecked car, cursing. He was badly shaken, and lurched when he walked.

Through the trees, on a crest of a hill, he could see the lights of the following car coming towards them rapidly. He turned and dragged Marie out of the car.

"Not a sound," he said, his gun digging into her side.

She stood close to him, her body shivering with shock and cold, and they both watched the lights come nearer. Faintly the wail of a siren split the air.

Raven showed his teeth. It was a Federal car, then. He waited, holding his breath as the lights grew larger. Then with a snarl and a roar the car swept past the turning he had taken and roared on into the night.

Raven relaxed limply. He wiped the cold sweat off his face. "Come on, you," he said to Marie, "we've got a little walk on."

Then, as she moved slowly towards the car, he suddenly realized that he couldn't take her any further. Now was the time to finish her, not later.

In the misty moonlight he could see her tall white body with its graceful lines, and again he wanted her. Throwing caution aside, he took two quick steps towards her and pulled her round. She gave a gasp of terror when she realized what he was going to do. She began to struggle and he was startled at her strength. They swayed together on the uneven ground and then she began to scream.

Raven broke away and swung his fist. It landed on her cheek-bone, high up. She staggered and, still screaming, fell to the ground. Raven knelt at her side, pinning her flat. "Shut up!" he said, gripping her arms viciously. "Make another sound an' I'll finish you."

She stopped screaming, but she still fought, twisting and pulling, trying to get free.

He said, "Lie still. Do you hear—damn you? Lie still."

She went limp suddenly, throwing her arms wide. One of her hands touched a heavy stone and her fingers closed round it. She tried to get the stone out of the ground.

Something was happening to her. She said: "No—no—no—" But one of his hands gripped her throat, and then, with a tremendous effort, she swung the stone wildly and hit him violently on the side of his head.

21

January 3rd, 11.45 p.m.

Snow fell heavily, but there was quite a crowd outside the State Prison gates.

Hogarty and Jay pushed their way through and showed their passes to the guard. They were glad to get inside for warmth.

Jay said, "It gets me why the hell those guys come to stand outside."

Hogarty took off his coat. "They're hopin' to catch a glimpse of the executioner. They don't know, but they haven't got a chance. He comes in a side entrance."

Jay looked round the bare room nervously. "I'll be mighty glad when this is over," he said. "I never liked executions."

Hogarty shrugged. "It'll be a pleasure to see a rat like that burn," he said. "I wouldn't miss it for anything."

"It's a long time ago, isn't it?" Jay said. "At least, it seems like it to me."

Hogarty nodded. "Come on and meet Davies. I know him quite well."

Jay hesitated. "Davies? You mean the executioner?"

"Yeah. Quite a guy. Come on an' meet him."

Jay followed him out of the room. One of the guards nodded to Hogarty. "What do you want, pal?" he said.

"Goin' along to see Davies," Hogarty said.

The guard told him where to go.

The execution-shed was across the courtyard, but they went round to it by a long passage and came in through a back door.

As they entered the little room Jay felt a slight sinking feeling. The chair stood opposite several wooden pews. A tall, thin man was standing by the chair, watching an electrician working. He glanced up when Hogarty crossed the room. His worn face lit up a trifle when he saw Hogarty. He shook hands. "This is your case, ain't it?" he said.

Hogarty nodded. "I want you to meet Ellinger," he said. "Ellinger, this is Davies."

Jay shook hands.

"Ellinger was the guy who first got on to Raven. He's one of us now," Hogarty explained.

"Some case," Davies remarked, chewing his long moustache. "I got a kick out of readin' about it in the tabloids. You know, I'm glad I'm going to be the guy who sends him over. I've never felt more convinced that a man deserves this as this guy does. Some of those dames he handled had a mighty bad time of it."

"Well, they avenged themselves all right. That Leroy dame caught him. We'd lost him all right when we heard shots, and when we got to them there she was half crazy, stark naked, running round in circles and he lying there knocked silly. Believe me, if she hadn't popped with the gun, we'd have gone past."

Davies grunted. He turned back to the chair. "I've just got to test this, if you boys'll excuse me."

The electrician handed him a board on which were a number of electric light bulbs. He put the board across the arms of the chair and then went over to the switch.

"Know anythin' about this, mister?" he asked.

Jay shook his head.

"Take the switch. It opens in oil. See? That prevents it sparking. We use 2,000 volts. Now watch." He turned the switch away from him. The bulbs across the chair-arms flashed up. "That means the juice is goin' through all right. It's the only way to test the current. Okay, Joe," he said to the electrician. "You can disconnect."

He picked up a small suit-case and opened it. "I always bring my own electrodes." He took out a baseball helmet. "This is for the head. I've got an electrode in here, and, as you can see, the helmet is lined with sponge. The sponge is moistened with a saline solution. It stops burning. You gotta watch all that. You gotta watch sparks as well. Wouldn't do to have burning an' sparks; upsets the witnesses."

He went over to the bucket and moistened the sponge.

Hogarty said in a low voice, "I guess we'd better sit down. The witnesses will be in in a minute."

They took up their positions in the last pew. Jay said, "This is giving me a guts-ache."

Before Hogarty could answer the door opened and a number of solemn-faced people filed in. There was a little confusion as they selected their seats.

Jay said suddenly, "For God's sake," and pointed with his eyes.

Sadie Perminger had just come in. She stood in the doorway, hesitating for a moment, and then she walked quickly to the front pew and sat down.

Jay had only a brief flash of her face, which was cold and bitter. She was dressed in black with a little black-and-white hat.

"How the hell did she get here?" Jay whispered.

"Raven asked her. You know the condemned can ask one person to see him go. Well, he asked her."

Jay stared at him.

"Maybe he thought it would amuse her," Hogarty said dryly.

Jay half looked over his shoulder. "They're coming," he said.

Down the corridor they could hear the steady tramp of feet. The door swung open and two guards came in. Raven walked after them. The minister and the Warden came last.

Raven looked round the small room and walked to the chair. His face was the colour of a fish's belly, but otherwise he seemed quite calm.

"That the guy?" he said, looking at Davies.

Davies came over to him and offered his hand. Raven looked at it, then shook hands.

"I'll get it over quick, son," Davies said in a low voice.

"Don't rush yourself," Raven said with a little sneer. "It's all the time I've got."

Two guards led him to the chair and he sat down.

The Warden came close to him and whispered. Raven said in a hard voice, "Sure, I'll say somethin'."

He looked slowly at each face in front of him, until his eyes met Sadie's. She looked at him with cold, implacable hatred, and he grinned.

"Well, boys," he said, still keeping his eyes on Sadie, "this is my last little speech. I've had a nice run for my money an' I ain't scared of goin'. You all know what my racket was. If you guys didn't want women, my racket wouldn't have lasted long. Don't forget that. All you smug-lookin' heels who've come to see me burn are as much to blame as I am. You get tired of your wives an' you want to have a fresh girl. So you come to me. That's all it is. The supply can't meet the demand. As long as you guys have the itch for a fresh girl, so will this racket go on. Nothin' can stop it. Cops certainly can't stop it. You can, but no one else. When you've all made up your minds to spend the rest of your nights with your wives, then girls won't have to trade their bodies. But you'll never do that. When I'm gone, someone else will take my place. There's always a demand and someone's gotta supply that demand."

He looked round the room again and then his eyes met Davies. "Come on, pal," he said, "get me outta here quick. These punks make me sick."

The guards, while he had been speaking, had already strapped him to the chair. Davies fixed the electrode to his leg and then swiftly the baseball helmet was fitted on his head.

Raven drew a long deep breath. "It's a pity I've got to leave my trains," he said. "Let her rip."

Davies had already stepped to the switch. He glanced at the Warden, who nodded. The switch went over and the lights dimmed. There came a sharp crackling sound and a whining cry of the current. Raven pitched forward, straining against the straps. A few sparks shot off the electrode on his leg, and a wisp of grey smoke appeared, coming from the top of the helmet.

Davies pulled the switch back so that Raven slumped limply in the chair, then, after a pause, the switch was thrown forward again. Raven once more plunged against the straps, only to sink back as the current was cut off.

Jay found he was trembling. He glanced over at Hogarty, who continued to chew, unmoved.

The doctor stepped forward and gingerly opened Raven's shirt. Jay could see the flesh bright red and sweating. With a towel the doctor wiped the sweat away, then with his stethoscope he listened for heart-beats.

He stood up. "I pronounce this man dead," he said.

The guards made signs for the witnesses to leave. As they were filing out Sadie suddenly turned back. Her face was still contorted with hatred, and now she looked a little mad. Before anyone could stop her she darted forward and spat in Raven's face.

CPSIA information can be obtained
at www.ICGtesting.com
Printed in the USA
LVHW091811270321
682674LV00003B/166